The Rock People of Sedona

A Spiritual Adventure

Rosemary Brown Sanders

Writers Club Press
San Jose New York Lincoln Shanghai

The Rock People of Sedona
A Spiritual Adventure

Published by Writer's Club Press,
an imprint of iUniverse.com, Inc.

For information address:
iUniverse.com, Inc.
620 North 48th Street
Suite 201
Lincoln, NE 68504-3467
www.iuniverse.com

To contact the author, write:
Rosemary Brown Sanders
P. O. Box 222872
Carmel, CA 93922-2872

ISBN: 1-893652-94-7

Printed in the United States of America

Contents

Acknowledgments

I'd like to thank my dearest friends, Patricia Bomont, Jeanette Quaglia, and Sally Winkleblack, for sharing this adventure with me.

To our husbands and children who graciously supported our need to explore the experiences leading to the writing of this book, we love you.

We'd like to honor both our dear editor and mentor, Ann West, whose skilled eyes and guided hands carefully edited the many manuscripts; and Kirk Bomont, for his publishing know-how and extreme patience.

We send our gratitude to the many colleagues, clients, and friends who have supported us along the way.

To our readers, it is our wish that you experience this book with a fresh curiosity and an open heart. Many blessings, and always remember:

"Angels see you as living light for that is what you really are."

Introduction

This story is a spiritual adventure. The participants, both human and non, create an incredible journey into an alternate existence. Nevertheless, the information in these pages can be applied to every life. A story within a story, it forms the fabric of magic at every turn.

Rojo, a tiny rock consciousness, arranges the many scenarios of this expedition and is responsible for our introduction to beings from other realities. Our journeys through time and space will inform, entertain, and introduce you to the possibility of consciously creating the future of mankind. You will also receive a warning: take better care of the planet, change your actions, and learn to create the world in which you wish to live. This is the urgent message for us all.

Within these pages you'll find the doorway to a wondrous universe existing simultaneously in the past, present, and future. The gracious hosts on the way are the aware beings of countless millennia who come forward to celebrate the universality of all life.

Now, it's your turn to open your mind to the world of the unseen, the part of life currently unknown to conscious belief. As a participant in this wonderful universe, allow yourself the opportunity to tap into the natural understanding of your human existence. We hope this tale you are about to embark upon will make your sojourn on Earth a little easier. And above all else, enjoy the spirit of the adventure.

*"What's an earth for
but to make a heaven of"*

—*Anonymous*

First Trip

1

Genesis One

It all started five years ago when we crowded into the small room, four ladies and myself, eagerly anticipating the voice of a spirit to entertain our questions.

We had been meeting weekly to receive the information and direction of various beings from the etheric realm and this was to be just another session. I, their channeler, sat in the deep-blue easy chair with my eyes closed, breathing heavily, drifting into trance.

Eventually a squeaky, high-pitched greeting proclaimed excitedly, "I am here. I am here."

I could sense my body reshaping itself, my shoulders scrunching toward my chest and my face feeling small and diminutive.

"My name is Rojo. I wish to invite you to visit my home in Sedona, Arizona. I feel it's safe for me, a mere rock, to speak to you because you, like we, are concerned about the outcome of the Earth.

"Please come to Sedona to help us and all who live upon us. Your interest in the ecology of the planet encourages you to touch base with the vortex energies, and I live where there are many of them. Will you come? Will you come soon?"

I snapped back into the room as his energy quickly left my body. The question was pleading...almost desperate...leaving us with a sense of urgency. None of us had channeled an inanimate object before. Wait a minute. Inanimate? This rock was far from inanimate. It had a charismatic personality, a high consciousness, and definite purpose.

Our initial impression of this unique visitor would lead us down an exceptional path, opening our minds to a world of newfound knowledge and a sense of unity beyond what we had ever experienced before. Our journey, Genesis One, had begun. We had committed to something unheard of…we had promised a rock we would make a trip to Sedona. So, plans had to be made. We knew timing was everything, and Rojo had assured us that all would be well.

The five of us—Jeanette, Patricia, Sally, Crystal, and myself—were excited beyond belief. This was to be our first long-distance outing together. Just imagine! Endless cosmic encounters with Rojo and various human and non-human intelligences, channeling the night away without interruption. What fun!

The scenery from the Phoenix airport to Sedona was much different from that on the cool Monterey Peninsula. This was definitely desert. Saguaro cactus lined the highway, their prickly arms seeming to wave at us. Some had individual personalities of their own and others were like small families, grouping themselves in various cozy arrangements. It was an amusing, friendly greeting.

Two-thirds of the way there, we spotted the rest stop Rojo had told us would signal the beginning of our journey. Searching the horizon for glimpses of our final destination, we suddenly received a channeling update. "You have arrived at the area and, without realizing it, constructed a five-pointed star symbolizing the energy of new beginnings. Your presence has created a beam of light penetrating the innerEarth and bouncing up into space, notifying the space beings of your arrival. Congratulations. You have followed the subliminal directions accurately. Welcome."

The drive into Sedona was unlike any other we'd seen. Towering red-rock formations rose before us, awesome in their luminescence. The majesty of the scene was so totally different from the desert through which we had just driven that a reverent hush overtook our previously chatty conversation. We felt right at home.

The first intersection we took note of was "Rojo Road." This coincidence was too great to ignore. Our rock friend had made sure we'd know we were in the right place at the right time. And the guidepost marking the location of the Coconino National Forest reminded Jeanette of her first missing-time experience when she was three years old. But that story is yet to come.

As we drove past Bell Rock and into the small quaint town of Sedona, a fuzzy brown creature darted across the road, alarming Sally and quickening her attention toward the highway ahead. Unbeknownst to us, this squirrel and others like him would play a significant part in our adventure.

*   *   *

Later that evening Rojo's bright voice announced, "I knew you had arrived because the land began to hum with your presence. I informed all of my Rock Rollers that you were indeed going to come, and they told me, 'Rojo, those people will not come so many miles from their home just to talk to you. You are only just a rock. They won't be interested in what you have to say.'"

"When you finally arrived I said, 'Ha ha, they are here. I told you so.' And that is when I promoted myself from Rock Roller to Ambassador of the Rocks. I knew you would come because it was in your hearts to know more about the earth energies, extraterrestrials, and the Rock People of Sedona.

"Tomorrow we will begin our adventure together, so for now, may your dreams be filled with the spirit of this place. Nighty nite."

2

Timing Is Everything

"Go to the bookstore." Rojo's persistent whispering inside my head was all I could hear the next morning. "Timing is everything."

I knew the importance of timing, but to convince everyone to take a giant leap into the unknown was something else again. By now we had become accustomed to the strange goings-on of "our company," the guides and mentors from the other side asking us to do what at times seemed impossible.

The Golden Word bookstore is a mainstay for New Age seekers in Sedona. People from everywhere on the planet stop in, some for directions and others to fulfill their questions about vortexes, hiking, and so on. The five of us, wide-eyed and wondering, trickled through the door and were soon swept up in books, gems, posters, and other mystical paraphernalia.

It had been a long while since I'd seen anything created by Patrick Flannigan, the young scientist who had helped develop the energy generators he called the neurophone and the sensor. Jeanette was familiar with his work also, so when I picked up a bottle of crystal-charged water I just had to blurt out, "Look what Flannigan's come up with now!" Brimming with curiosity, Jeanette ran over to see my discovery, and at that instant an unfamiliar yet pleasant voice behind us said, "If you think that's new, you should see what else he has."

Jeanette avidly took up the discussion with the interested stranger, leaving me to escape into the racks of books.

I'm always mesmerized by places like this, and my mind wandered away from the stranger as I explored all the magic. I was deep in concentration when I heard the tinkle of the bell on the front door. Just then, the clerk behind the counter said to Jeanette, "You really should take him up on his invitation. He has the only round, red-domed house in the area. You'll see something special, and he doesn't extend such an invitation to everyone." Sure enough, Jeanette was holding a hand-scribbled map the quiet stranger had drawn.

"Time to leave," Rojo's voice guided me. I rushed my friends one by one out of the store and into the car. As usual, Sally was raring to go, to get on the road, to find the vortexes. And from that moment on, everything became a blur.

"Don't go too far," Rojo cautioned. "You must visit the round house today. Don't forget. It's important."

"Yeah, right," the critical part of my mind nagged. "We're supposed to drop everything, go out of our way, and visit a total stranger. And besides that, he lives in the middle of nowhere." "Don't worry," was the patient reply. "You will be safe. We've arranged this meeting for you. Trust the Rock People and continue to listen. If it's meant to be, you'll each hear the message simultaneously and agree to it at once. You will know when it's time."

For the rest of the morning we oriented ourselves with the area, eventually deciding to have a quickie lunch. Sure enough, when we finished eating we became very quiet and could think of nothing else but to find the round red house. It was a compelling, karmic kind of feeling. We had to get there, and it had to be soon.

Sally swung the car out of the restaurant parking lot and, armed with our hand-drawn map, we sped westward on a wing and a prayer. We found the dirt road indicated on the map and with it, each pothole. Eyeing the mile markers, we came to a fork in the road. "Let's see, it doesn't show a split. Now what?"

We peered out of the dust-encrusted windows to be met by a red cow standing in the middle of the left fork, blocking the road. Once again we were being led; our decision seemed to have been made for us. Trekking down the rugged lane, we passed a windmill, and around a final curve, the prominent red geodesic house welcomed us.

"We're here," our fivesome sang out on cue as the rental car doors slammed behind us.

We were greeted by the gentle, kind man from the bookstore who I noticed had an intriguing rainbow aura. "Come in, I'm so glad you could make it. Let me show you around."

The interior design of the structure executed pure symmetry. The ceiling itself was 20-feet high in the center of the living room. A concave skylight edified the enormous crystals, shooting rainbows onto the stucco walls.

"Ready for the tour?" he smiled, motioning us into single file. We negotiated the spiral staircase to the second floor where a bathroom and bedroom were featured. More circular windows allowed streams of light into various spaces, framed with Native American decor. After a few minutes, he left us on our own to explore the rest of the house, excusing himself and returning with glasses of lemonade. We sat in the living room listening to stories of his passion for Sedona and his first-hand encounters with the many kinds of spaceships he'd seen.

"If you have a moment, I'd like to show you a special place. We don't have much time before the sun sets, but if we hurry, it will be worth it."

We were eager to explore the mystery of the canyons, so we excitedly agreed.

"Better take your car and follow me so you can find your way there again if you feel like returning."

Our cars sped off, trailing dust on our way to unknown treasures lying in wait. We parked as close as possible to the wall of towering Boynton Canyon, where trees had already eclipsed the sun from the entrance.

Hurriedly we scrambled up the canyon paths until we found ourselves on a pointed shelf facing the setting sun. Before us hung the "windows of heaven," a natural, weathered formation rounded into the wall of the canyon. It reminded me of the medicine wheel circle of the sacred Earth. There we gathered, hand in hand, and prayed for the world and the divine soul of spirit that had led us there.

We were now firmly launched on our adventure. From this kismet meeting with our new friend, Jason, we would go on to hike Sedona's canyons, discuss UFO area sightings, merge with spirits of the Anasazi Indians, and greet fellow light seekers on the path. It was magical...it was cosmic...it was meant to be. We knew it, Jason knew it, Rojo knew it, and the cow in the road must have known it, too.

When we left, it was dark and late. We searched the skies for signs of the UFOs Jason had encouraged us to find—cigar-shaped crafts, saucers, and mother ships. The stars seemed so close, maybe because there was no competition from city lights.

"You and the sky are one. We are not alone," the Rock People whispered. "From now on you will all be able to think together as one. Welcome to OUR world."

* * *

Sally had gathered some herbs in Boynton Canyon the day before, stuffing the treasures into her back-pack. That morning the sage omelet tasted terrific. Perhaps it was psychological, but I'd like to think our love of the land was the reason.

We'd been up late the night before, channeling until the witching hour of 3:00 a.m., but our energy level was surprisingly high despite the lack of sleep. Today it was off to the vortexes to perform an initiation with key symbols we had been given before leaving home. We reached the lower Airport Mesa area and found it filled with pink and red jeep tours. Unlike Boynton Canyon, which yesterday was sparse with tourists, this place was like Grand Central Station. As soon as we'd find a quiet area, a tour group would catch up with us. When we finally had a moment alone, there was such an overwhelming sense of negative energy that we decided it must be time to use the key symbols for a healing. We drew the secret symbols in the crusted red soil, but, dogged by the tour groups, we kept our ceremony short and quiet.

The idea to leave the tourist-packed area felt right. We scrambled into the car only to be interrupted by a loud tapping on the window. A slender tour guide bent down and peered in. In his hand was a small, white shiny button.

"Did one of you ladies lose this?" he queried. None of us had, but he insisted we take it anyway, that it must belong to us. There had been at least 50 or 60 other people traipsing through the trails, but the man wouldn't take no for an answer. Somehow he was very different, emanating a strange, rather dissimilar vibration. He had left his paid customers to fend for themselves in order to "rightfully" return a button that wasn't ours in the first place.

I held the little button as we sat dumbfounded. Scratching our heads, we had to laugh. "This is a gift," the little voice said, "an acknowledgement of your prayer work for the vortex. It is one of the symbols, is it not?"

Lo and behold it formed the circle of life: the eyes of the giver, the ears of the receiver. "It is most significant. Now go to the airport terminal for lunch. We have more to show you."

"More? More what?"

"You shall see. Life is like a button—bright and shiny. You shall see."

* * *

The five of us crammed ourselves into the booth at the airport restaurant. It wasn't the most elegant atmosphere in the world but maybe the "down homiest," especially the dog-eared appearance of the menu. The iced tea sounded great considering the stifling heat and absence of air conditioning.

A short time after we had ordered, Rojo put me on alert. "They are coming, they are coming. They are here!" Just then, two tall, thin human-looking beings rounded the corner and headed toward the table next to us. Even though one was male and the other female, they appeared to be duplicates of each other wearing matching jumpsuits. They walked in sync together, rather stiffly, and sat down at precisely the same time. A few moments later, an older man came in and sat with them, but they said nothing to each other. They all ordered pie and coffee.

I was prompted to check it out with Rojo. "Are these the ones? Am I right that they have no human vibrational field?"

"Quite right," Rojo replied. "They are not from this world. They are here studying the area. They are flight masters or astronauts, you might say."

I nudged Jeanette with anticipation. "Are they ETs? What do you think?"

She looked at them expectantly. "Yes, look at their skin...it's so smooth...and perfect."

I looked over Jeanette's shoulder and my attention was drawn to two men in suits, dark suits, in 90 degree weather. Their jackets were still on and they were watching our every move. I was increasingly aware that we were the only human customers in the whole restaurant. "Rojo," I asked, "are those men in suits also ETs?"

"Yes, they are observing you now and seeing what you're up to."

As I turned back to the young man in the jumpsuit, he stood up and faced the table. Had he read my mind? I'd wanted to get his attention, to talk to him.

The camera! It was on the table. Hurriedly I picked it up and asked him to take our picture. As he examined the device like he'd never seen one before, I noticed the name on his jumpsuit. Kohoutek it said. Good one, I thought to myself, now I'll break the ice. "Do you know you have the same name as the comet?" I asked shyly. He looked down at the word as if reading it for the first time and nodded.

He took the picture and silently handed back the camera with an obviously practiced smile. Then the twins left at the same time...step in step, stiffly, awkwardly. They had neither touched their pie nor drunk their coffee. The men in the dark suits took off right after them. Then it hit me! Why did I ask him to take our picture? We should have taken theirs!

Leaving the little restaurant, bewildered but thrilled, we noticed a carefully framed newspaper article hanging in the waiting area. The headline read, "Amelia Earhart Abducted by UFOs." The clipping was from the '40s and speculated that hers had been the ultimate abduction. After lunching with these extraterrestrials, I wondered if this was to be our fate as well, but Rojo reassured me, "We are all one—even the visitors. Remember, we are all just visiting."

3

Visiting the Vortexes

"Castle Rock, Castle Rock," Rojo kept repeating over and over in my mind.

"But I've checked all the maps and there's no place called Castle Rock," I countered.

"It has spires...three of them. Get in the automobile and we will direct you."

Many times we had hopped in the car and let Rojo do the navigating, so this was not out of the ordinary. As we drove, my mind attempted to recall the previous night's channeling about processes for healing. Darn it, why couldn't I remember all that pristine information as it had been given? Those clicking and snapping noises I was now hearing were surely meant not only to heal us, but also to guide us.

As Rojo dictated directions to Sally, we made our way to a site the locals call Cathedral Rock. This must be what Rojo had meant. Sure enough, a three-spired formation arose from the horizon looking just like a medieval castle. We found a parking space on the road and headed up the crowded path. This is not a secluded spot, I thought to myself. It's difficult to receive information with a lot of other people around, but if this was where Rojo wanted us, so be it.

We hiked for a long time, waiting for a sign. "Is anyone getting any information?" I asked.

"No, not really," was the disappointed reply. We'd been there close to an hour and not a peep. Maybe we should be somewhere else, my critical mind proposed.

When I saw the beer cans strewn around and teenagers splashing in the river, I realized it was the college spring break. Maybe that's why I wasn't getting any instructions. We were all eager to find something…anything…any tiny bit of vibration to tell us if we were on the right track. We started back down the trail, dejected at the thought of spending so much time without results.

I've often experienced the ups and downs of spirit communication— data elaborately executed through intermittent puzzle pieces despite all the frustration of surrounding circumstances. Like the time, years ago, when my girlfriend in Los Angeles wanted to meet John Travolta. We had set the energy by thinking positively, knowing that only the highest intention must be held in order to contact him. It takes two to tango, so to speak, to arrange etherically an agreed-upon time and place and then bring this kind of meeting to reality.

One weekend, we took off to Santa Barbara to enact the feat armed with our pendulums, maps, guides, and good intentions. Our guidance was that she would meet him by a roadside stand of some sort. He would be driving a cream-colored Mercedes SL and be with a friend. Wow! With all this information it should have been a snap, right? Not exactly.

We spent all day driving up one mountain and down the next, stopping at every fruit, vegetable, pottery, coffee, and magazine stand we could find. Once we had exhausted ourselves, we made our way back home. Two tanks of gas and an enormous amount of time and energy had been consumed listening to inner direction…for nothing. Why would the next day be any different?

"Trust," was the answer. "Just trust."

Yes, I knew it could be done. I'll never forget the magic of the next day in Los Angeles when I left work, drove to my friend's house, and begged her to accompany me. That afternoon I trusted the voices and the direction. We followed my guidance for hours—streetlight by streetlight, corner by corner—until we reached a little-known terminal on the reverse side of the Burbank airport.

I parked the car in front of a large palm tree and took out a red pen and a rubber band—the perfect ingredients to construct a home-made pendulum. "He's coming," the inner voice said. "This is the place."

My friend was obviously discouraged from the day before. "Ah, come on," I pleaded. "Trust me." The pendulum was swinging wildly, yet my words fell on deaf ears.

"How long do we have to sit here?" was her sullen response.

"Look, the pendulum's moving. He's on his way!"

"Not again," she moaned.

In my mind I heard, "Hold on...he's coming," and, glancing into the rear-view mirror, I noticed a cream-colored Mercedes SL turn into the driveway the wrong way. I recognized the driver immediately.

"He's here!" I heard my mind shout. "It's him!" I whispered out loud. "See for yourself!"

How dare I ever question after that day when we did meet him just as the universe had arranged. My mind wandered to the same feeling of dejection here in Sedona. We'd come a long way, made all the arrangements, but there was no message. Trust. It all came back to that word defined in the dictionary as "a firm belief in the honesty, integrity, and reliability of another person or thing; faith."

Then I remembered. The channeling the night before was all about using the body to heal...that by snapping your fingers and rubbing your hands together you can affect your body. Just then a strange clicking began. It became louder and louder until it was the only sound I could hear. "STOP!" I shouted. "They want us to wait here." Everyone else could hear it by now, too.

The thought came through from Rojo, "Healing. That's the next step." Then he continued, "Don't leave this area yet. Turn left. You will see a rock and a frog. Go there now."

A narrow concrete bridge lay to the left and, sure enough, beyond that a big rock shaped like a frog. Into the riverbed we stepped, making our way toward the rock. Incredible! There sat a little white frog, sunning itself in the middle of the day. This was a sign of what we had come there to experience—a healing.

The rest of the afternoon we took turns lying on the large warm rock, being healed and experiencing the wonder of it all. Then, taking off our shoes and dipping our feet into gentle Oak Creek, we joyfully tossed tiny crystals into the twinkling water as "thank yous" to our spirit friends.

The sun was signaling late afternoon so we gathered our belongings and turned to retrace our steps. "Rock Rollers! Rock Rollers!" I heard in my head. Rojo had gifts for each of us, tiny rock images that would magically roll out in front of us as we walked the trail. Amazing.

"Pick up the first one you see in the middle of the path," was his instruction. "It's yours, made for you by the elements, crafted by the rock beings as a memento of your experience here."

As we strolled along, the carved rocks rolled one by one onto the path ahead. Jeanette received a miniature UFO; Sally, a Mother Mary; Patricia, a human face; and Crystal, a soaring hawk. The symbols meant something special to each of us personally. Mine was perfect, an image I'd collected since I was sixteen years old—a mother and child. How could the Rock People have known? Little did I realize that they knew even more about the relevance of this image than I did.

* * *

Just before sunset we arrived at Bell Rock, crimson-etched against the sky. It was probably too late to be experiencing another energy vortex; but time, like the sun, has a way of shadowing itself in Sedona. We left the car and began our approach to the imposing red mound.

Sally's intense desire to become one with the rock led her to hike boundlessly up the natural bell to the very top. The rest of us were prepared to follow, but one of our spirit guides, Screeching Hawk, had different plans. The presence of his energy on the plateau was so noticeable that we just stood there spellbound.

Before long, the rest of us felt inspired to collect nearby pieces of rock and form a circle for ceremony. A soft wind whirled up around us in singular contrast to the acute silence. In the next moment, Screeching Hawk spoke, his message spilling into our consciousness. He wanted us to listen to everything in the universe, and he introduced us to Talking Tree, leaning precariously out of an adjacent rock. The elderly spruce, gnarled and twisted from top to roots, creaked a confirmation at his every word.

Indeed, the spirit of this wise Indian warrior was telling us, through the mechanism of channeling, of new beginnings, spiritual journeys, and co-creation. We were mesmerized by his words as they touched our souls and echoed in the wind and sky.

Then, suddenly, Screeching Hawk was quiet. I felt his energy rush toward Sally on the mound, holding her very essence. Something's wrong. Just moments before, he had named her "Running Deer" because of her fire to reach the peak and return before the sun could disappear.

Screeching Hawk's voice had faded into the wind, but I now detected a faraway sensation. Looking as through his eyes, I soared closer and closer with him to the mountain…searching, waiting, and watching for a sign that all was well. It wasn't. His focus traveled to Sally as she hung, precariously suspended between a gaping crevice and a steep, sheer cliff. This was serious. One move in either direction might send her plummeting down the side of Bell Rock. The danger of the moment became a stark reality.

My attention turned to the presence of beings from a different time and space hovering over Sally in a brilliant stream of light. I was able to feel those iridescent shimmering faceless bodies somehow giving her comfort. I became aware that a sense of total acceptance had now filled her being. An all-encompassing desire to commune with this presence came over me, and my fear for her safety gradually began to wane.

Her decision to ascend the crevice had been made. Arms and legs quivering, Sally carefully inched her body backwards up the face of the giant rock until she reached the safety of the jagged ledge. Those elegant forms of light protected her from every side, attended by her own guardian angel. At that very instant, a blanket of peace fell over her and she knew she was not alone. United with the fearless spirit of Screeching Hawk, she heard the Four Winds humming a song of love.

Once again on solid ground, she reverently offered gifts to the light ones and elders who had lifted her safely into the arms of the Great Spirit. With gratitude, she ceremoniously placed tiny crystals from the pouch around her neck into the openings on the rocks. She felt a thousand unseen eyes acknowledge her gifts. It seemed all too small a token for the life she had almost surrendered to the giant monolith.

Just as suddenly as Screeching Hawk had stopped talking, he picked up again mid-sentence where he had left off. He confirmed that Sally was safe, after which the four of us said a silent prayer of thanks. As the coolness descended, we also expressed our deepest desires and wishes to the universe.

"Birth new beginnings. Start anew. Your life is in your own hands. Let the seeds be planted and the unfolding begin."

Screeching Hawk's prophetic words would touch each of us profoundly in the months to come. Our lives were indeed about to change…although none of us realized quite how much.

*   *   *

That evening we were gifted with the presence of a unique guide previously introduced to us by Rojo as his mentor.

"This is Moha, Elder of the Rock People. Screeching Hawk has asked me to take you on a spiritual journey through Bell Rock."

[Note: This visualization can be read aloud to you by another person, recorded on tape, or a copy purchased from Rosemary Brown Sanders. See the back of this book.]

Bell Rock Visualization

Allow yourself to relax. Breathe deeply and fully and leave old thought patterns behind. Free yourself of thoughts of doubt, or fear, or negativity, for the journey will be difficult enough without carrying the load of things you no longer need.

Standing at the base of Bell Rock looking skyward, the beauty of the heavens calls to you. The stillness and grandeur of the rock, the colors—orange, tan, rust, red, yellow, and ivory—emit healing energy that fills your soul with goodness. Use these colors to cleanse your body, to heal it, to warm it.

See the colors of Bell Rock in you and begin to climb safely and easily up the base of the mountain, noticing the various energies that exist there...the essence of the Indians, the sacred ones who once lived at the foot of the mountain. Feel their beingness. Hear their haunting cries and dance on the petals of the moon. Listen to the wind as it speaks through the talking tree, calling out your name and inviting you to go higher onto the plateau of my people, the Rock People.

We welcome you. We honor your love and your knowledge. We call to you like a mother's beating heart calls to her infant. Let us take you through the secret chambers of the mountain.

An opening in the rock appears before you. Simply make your way through this opening into the vastness of the caverns, into the beauty of the rock, into the space known as the Sacred Mountain that connects the Belt of Orion to the Earth plane. Here lie many rings of truth and light and knowledge, much like those of Saturn. The rings exist for you to walk upon and from which to gain knowledge.

As you move in a circular pattern, feel yourself navigate the spiral of life, gradually going higher and higher. As you travel upward, reach to the top of the mountain, to the spires. Journeying up the sacred steps, you find yourself atop Bell Rock looking down at the beauty below, at the majesty of all life...plants, rocks, clouds, and sky.

Look upward and see the angels there to greet you. They support...surround...and hold you. Feel now the waves of Orion flow downward through the heavens, falling gently around you. A spiral of energy descends from this space. Fill yourself with this energy, your connectedness to the star systems, for Orion has much to say to you.

You can learn about the pyramids, the sacred geometry of Earth, and the Rock People. Their forms and shapes are not by chance but planned individually by families and ancestors like your own kind, with great genetic structuring. You belong to everything. Part of your heart and soul belongs to the sky and the universe, and the other part belongs to the land, to your Earth. You share the best of both worlds, you believe in both heaven and Earth...for as above, so below.

Let your memories of Bell Rock to return to you in the most comfortable way possible, for the journey you have just taken has been great. The rocks you have touched and walked upon have felt the divine presence of the Master as well as many other etheric beings who are dedicated to making this a more enlightened world in which to be.

Now, the angels are flying you around Bell Rock to see the beauty and feel the energy, connecting you with the Rock People. You can see Rojo at the very top...waving. There are tears in his little rock eyes because his love for you is complete in every way. By your coming, you have melted his heart.

Now, gradually, let your thoughts return you to the room in which you are sitting. With each breath, feel yourself returning to your body; and when you are ready, slowly open your eyes.

4

Healing the Past

After leaving Bell Rock we were ravenous and rejoiced to hear that Jeanette knew of the perfect natural-food place just down the road. When we spotted the "Home Cookin" sign, we parked and made a beeline for the door.

The rustic coffee shop was oddly decorated with spurs and saddles on the walls but, relying on Jeanette's culinary expertise, we straddled the benches beside a long linoleum-topped table in the back. Our hunger obscured the lack of usual accommodations and we quickly turned our attention to the menu. We assumed it would be packed with tasty regional delicacies. In our dreams! Chili, chitlins, southern-fried chicken and biscuits, chicken-fried steak…we read on and on. Aghast, we searched for more nouveau cuisine. They must at least have the basics, like salad and baked potatoes. No baked? Only mashed? Okay. How about a side of baby green beans? And perhaps, a slice of berry cobbler? Perplexed by the limits of the menu choices, we nevertheless hastily ordered.

After every encounter with spirit energy we love to rehash (oops, poor choice of words at this eatery) and discuss everything we've just experienced. And thus we began to share the amazing happenings of the day we'd just spent with our elemental friends. When our food arrived, however, we stopped short to ponder our mystery meals—the dull, army-green appearance of the canned green beans and the chemical taste of instant potatoes. But this wouldn't be the half of it.

As we took our first bites of food in too many hours, we suddenly noticed a change in Jeanette. She had an enormous mouthful...but she wasn't swallowing. Her puffy cheeks resembled a chipmunk storing nuts for the winter, and her hands were awkwardly holding on to her fork and searching for her mouth. Behind the food, a husky voice muttered something like, "This child needs sustenance."

More food was going in, but no chewing was taking place. Then, to our astonishment, she reached into her mouth and pulling out chunks of partially gnawed beef, replaced them on her plate. Next came the sound of intense breathing and then the laugh...the huge, uproarious laughter! "Oh no. Not here. Not now," I pleaded.

Too late...it could only be Samuel, Jeanette's exclusive spirit guide from childhood. It takes only a small opening of her heart to awaken Samuel to this dimension. We were sure everyone in the restaurant had noticed, but they all sat still as if levitating within another world, oblivious to the obvious.

By now, Jeanette had totally left her body and Samuel had taken her place. When Samuel enters, Jeanette etherically expands out of her tiny frame into his immense seven-foot proportions. Samuel loves to talk with his hands, using enormous gestures and putting at risk all items within reach. We scurried to move everything out of the way and hurriedly gulped our food, knowing we must move Jeanette out of the restaurant as quickly as possible or be perceived as the epitome of California's nuts and flakes.

We decided to split up. Two of us would take her to the car and the others would hurry next door to buy groceries for breakfast. Whatever we did, it had to be fast. We flew out of the coffee shop with the management in pursuit, afraid we might not pay our bill. But even through the whir of commotion, we managed to pay the tab and order the berry cobbler to go.

In our rush to get home, Patricia sprained her ankle on the walkway to the condo. Immediately Jeanette, as Samuel, dropped down and began a healing. We stood outside for the 10-minute session, after which Patricia miraculously walked the rest of the way without pain.

Minutes later, huddled in the condo hallway with Samuel's long, expansive arms around the four of us, we listened to his blessings and the why of our existence. We felt the love of this beautiful guide and the true joy of being in Sedona together.

*   *   *

All through our trip squirrel messengers were amongst us. On this next day we began to detect more "signs" delivered by these unassuming little creatures. They would run across the road, especially when we needed to slow down and see what the universe was trying to say. I remembered that in Jamie Sams' Medicine Cards the squirrel honors the future and signals the possibility of change. Squirrels also remind us that perhaps we carry too much baggage around with us in this world.

Undoubtedly, we were getting ready to lighten our load, to release everyday, ordinary ways of being…to venture out further beyond boundaries. "Carry only the wisdom, let go of all fear," the squirrel messengers warned. We began to acknowledge our furry friends who helped us experience the totems of the animal spirits here in this beautiful place.

Squirrels were everywhere, triggering our curiosity and attention to the past. As if guided by them, we felt our combined synergistic energy as we drove through the Coconino National Forest. In fact, Jeanette was so moved by their appearance that recurring images from long ago popped into her mind. She'd told us before of a missing-time episode that happened when she was only three years old. While playing with her cousins in the rural setting of her Montana home, she had mysteriously disappeared. Her entire family searched frantically for her, and three hours later she was found in her little white dress…now quite dirty…still in the ravine where the children had originally been playing.

Many times during her young life, Jeanette would point to airplanes flying overhead and pronounce, "Coconino, Coconino," her own childhood term for describing a vehicle in flight. Jeanette once told this story to a psychiatrist. While under hypnosis, she answered many questions about the incident. When she came out of the trance state, she noticed her doctor was visibly shaken and wouldn't discuss the incident. He also chose not to give her the tape of their session because he thought it was "too weird...too sensitive."

Having nature all around, plus hearing the name of the forest, triggered a subliminal need in Jeanette to search for the truth. Quite honestly, the vortex energy of Sedona is so powerful that many people come just to be healed, either by the rocks or the well-qualified healers who gravitate to this place.

We asked our friend Jason for a recommendation and he suggested we call Dr. Lipari who lives out of town about an hour away. Sally and I agreed to drop off Jeanette, Patricia, and Crystal first and then head toward the Tooziegoot Monument to explore on our own.

Opening the screen door to Dr. Lipari's office, we were greeted by a blue-eyed Husky wearing a red bandana around his neck. The dog invited us in as if we were old friends. We spent a while in a waiting area filled with colorful paintings of dolphins and extraterrestrial landscapes. Past the looming image of Albert Einstein, I glimpsed a view of a freestanding, five-foot copper pyramid occupied by an elderly Native American. As my eyes met his, an unspoken communication revealed our soul connection from another lifetime. My gaze was interrupted by the soothing voice of an obviously gentle soul as Dr. Lipari introduced himself and his dog.

"Hello, we're glad you're here," he said, gesturing to include the big silver dog. "Who's first?"

Jeanette eagerly stepped forward. She was ready...ready for one of the most moving and meaningful cosmic experiences of her life.

Jeanette's session with the kind doctor would trip many blocked circuits, cascading her through countless memories locked within her mind. He launched her into different dimensions populated by holograms and quintessential beings where she saw herself traveling to various planets on spaceships...the same "Coconino" ships she had been taken aboard when she was a little girl. She was finally being treated to the lost knowledge she had yearned to discover since childhood.

While all this was going on, Sally and I manifested our own uncommon encounters at Tooziegoot. The monument stuck out perpendicular to the straight road. One of the largest remaining pueblos in the region, it was once part of the sophisticated culture that mysteriously flowered throughout meso-America. This interesting structure is completely made of rock and includes an off-site museum. We could sense the sacredness of the area despite the rustle of nearby tourists in campers and cars.

Inside the small museum, one can examine the tools and artifacts of a culture long removed. As we ascended the outer stairs, I felt the intense presence of Apache souls in the surrounding area. Moved by these spirits, I asked Sally to drive to a place beyond the monument where I was sensing the heaviness of a great battle. The feeling crescendoed until we spotted a beckoning graveyard. I suspected that many had died on this spot in the shadow of Tooziegoot. Because vivid pictures played like a movie in my head, I was able to share with her a scene of horses charging down the hill toward the armed settlers. I perceived the smell of smoke from firearms and the dust of hoofs. It was a terrible and bloody battle. Nearly everyone died there in the hot desert that desperate day a hundred or so years ago. Our hearts were heavy as we left.

We arrived a few minutes early to pick up Jeanette, Patricia, and Crystal and were asked to wait in the seating area. The Indian gentleman still sat in the same spot. I heard him mention being a chief, well over a hundred years old. He was concerned about the land and the lack of corn. His eyes were deep and longing...longing for the way of the past.

My mind connected with the voices of the Ancient Ones. The Anasazi had called Sedona "Wipuk," meaning "at the foot of sacred rock mountains." Now the ageless canyon took on a deeper meaning. Through the chief's thoughts, I began to envision the gleam of the "helmeted ones," Spanish intruders whom "the people of the Sun" had dreaded, usurping resources from this beautiful place. The old Indian's spirit voice faded back into the present as he thanked us for the friendly conversation.

Dr. Lipari's uncanny way of opening people to locked knowledge on the inner planes was sincerely appreciated by all three ladies. After he gave them a goodbye hug, he placed a dried corn kernel into the star of their palms saying, "This is from my friend, Chief Running Blue Bear, who enjoyed your kind company. May his spirit be there to guide you through life."

* * *

On the drive home, a strange recurring image was telepathically transmitted to my psyche. The American Indian in Dr. Lipari's office would smile and nod, his hands holding the kernels of dried corn about which he was speaking. Then, the kernels would fall from his hand, dropping to the base of a dead, twisted tree. I was very puzzled by this apparition until the spirit of the chief appeared to relay a personal telepathic message of help and hope for each of us.

I saw before me a huge white teepee, its flap wide open, decorated with Indian symbols—a half moon, a large pointed sun, some cornstalks, and a lightning bolt. Running Blue Bear began to speak through me.

"The abundance you seek is within. You have great knowledge of the ways of the Earth. The Great Spirit is taking care of you. As your laughter flows freely, so may abundant life.

"In order to create happiness, focus within. Do not let the elements distract you from your inner-life work. The lightning bolt on the teepee represents action and energy, causing reaction. The moon tells of the Grandmothers; the sun, of the Great Spirit; and the cornstalks, of growth and abundance.

"Think of yourself as a teepee wearing these symbols, and enter through the flap to see what lies in the open space. Feel the sense of who you are, for in order to be comfortable here you must learn to live with yourself. There is no need to remain outside, for once inside the teepee you can wonder about all things.

"Always be true to yourself for others can read self-doubt, lack of confidence, or fear. When you are not true, your thoughts will act like a repellant. You will be like the skunk within its lovely silken fur who does not allow one to get too close. Instead of emitting an odor, you emit a vibration…a scent of lack, anger, or not being understood. Therefore, go within so that you can face knowing who you are.

"When you put on your clothes or jewelry, you don't in any way change your real self. When you know who you are, you can touch all forms of life.

"In order to grow corn, you must re-harvest it. The corn that falls away from the stalk does not by itself create more corn. Only the kernels skillfully removed and dried will provide new stalks. To insure that your harvest is abundant, you must be willing to plant seeds. No matter how dry the land, your thoughts, like the seeds, are the way to create a plentiful harvest.

"Let go of that which is gathered unless it is collected through caring and wisdom. Set your mind and heart free…and everything will be taken care of in its own time."

* * *

We spent the next day in the Anasazi ruins above Boynton Canyon. We were delighted by the petroglyphs that pulsed with a powerful energy. Jason told us about the spirituality of these Indians who seemed to have disappeared into thin air, leaving only pottery shards and petroglyphs behind.

Crystal was having flashbacks, those deja vu feelings of a previous lifetime. Hurriedly she made her way to the burned-out kivas, or apartment-like enclosures, where the Anasazi had lived. She bent down to examine the carved, painted symbols that were centuries old, sensing the meaning of every one. Patricia, also, was lost in the magnificence of the canyon walls and sacred pools. The memory of ancient ceremony was mirrored at every turn.

We faced the setting sun over Boynton Canyon and together held hands in a circle, awakened to the memory of the canyon's past. Together we sang the "Spirit Welcome Song," an Indian prayer honoring the four directions, as our gift to the spirit people and rock beings of Sedona.

* * *

It was late and dark when we left the canyon and nothing but desert lay before us. Something comes over you when you are in Sedona. It's a stillness of sorts, a calling to reach up and out to the furthest stars. All I could think of was the fun we'd had. The elaborately arranged synchronistic happenings were too obvious to miss. Even if we had tried, we couldn't have planned the week better.

"Leave part of yourself behind." The little rock voice in my head startled me from my reverie.

"What do you mean?"

"You must leave a symbol of the wonder you have created here. The stars leave their light to shine every night. Use your imagination, but leave a part of yourselves behind."

The words were puzzling, but it had been a long day. Perhaps I was missing the point, veiled by the mystical nature of it all. Oh well, I would think about it and then let go. This is what I had been learning...to let go.

* * *

The shopping is rich in Sedona, a town with charming Indian stores, southwestern food-tasting shops, and a variety of goodies. It was a brand new day and I wanted something to take home...something beautiful. In and out of the gift shops we strolled. I sauntered along, looking back and forth hoping something would jump out at me...something I could fall in love with. The ladies were so patient. I've always thought everyone likes shopping as much as I do, but the rocks and beauty of Sedona were constantly urging Sally to hike up mountains and unearth more natural treasures. I knew I would have to hurry or lose the opportunity to fulfill my desires.

Rounding the corner of the curio shop, I spotted it...sleek, lovely, and serene. Its smooth contours were handcrafted in exquisite simplicity. Bursting with excitement, I picked up the sculpture...the head of a striking woman with a five-pointed star set atop her flowing hair. Underneath the form were the words, "Star Catcher." This was what I had been searching for.

* * *

That evening we had invited Jason out to dinner to say goodbye and thank him for his generosity. Just as we were about to step out the door, I received an urgent message from Rojo. "The Star Catcher is not for you," he cautioned. "It belongs to the man in the round red house. It's a symbol of all of you...the five-pointed star...the star you created as you stood outside the car when you first arrived in Sedona. It is the female essence of your beings. This is how you will say thank you and how you will leave a bit of yourselves behind."

Rojo was right. Star Catcher wasn't mine...it was ours. Ours to give away like a precious treasure that grows more valuable when offered with the heart.

"We're supposed to give this to Jason," I announced.

"Oh, yes!" Everyone agreed. "Let's include a little note."

Our note soon became a poetic verse conveying the joy of our journey. The deed was done. Star Catcher and the Rock People of Sedona would get their wish, and we were rewarded with the opportunity to collectively compose these heartfelt words to Jason.

> *In the beginning*
> *there were five*
> *who joined the one*
> *creating the whole*
> *connecting the universe.*
> *Your heart has sung a song*
> *that we knew as one of us*
> *in a soul link*
> *of All That Is.*

5

Winds of Change

After we arrived home, the months quietly drifted by and we vicariously relived the moments in Sedona again and again. During one of our weekly channeling sessions, I confided to my friends that I wasn't feeling well. I was always tired and had ongoing flu-like symptoms. Someone suggested I might be pregnant.

Pregnant? No way. I hadn't had a child in ten years. It couldn't be! My mind returned to Bell Rock and the words of Screeching Hawk. "This is a time of new beginnings…new birthings. All of the energies are now creating new life."

"Yes, but you must have been speaking of a spiritual rebirth, surely not a physical birth," I answered in my thoughts. Then I remembered the two-inch rocks Rojo had magically left as gifts for us. Mine had been a mother-and-child symbol because I collected them. My home was decorated with sculptures, icons, and paintings all representing the same theme.

Well, needless to say, nine months to the day we arrived home from Sedona, my own little miracle was born. We named him Rhyan, and he is truly my gift from God and the beings of Sedona.

* * *

Screeching Hawk's warning of "winds of change" was becoming more and more visible in our lives. Subtle changes had been occurring for each of us, but the shifts within Crystal were the most noticeable. I began to realize that our trip together had opened personal wounds for her that were in need of healing.

The catharsis she was undergoing was not unlike the rush of a kundalini experience. Because she was our elder, she was more concerned than the rest of us about the uncomfortable rapid heartbeat sensations she was experiencing since our return from Sedona. Therefore, she decided to leave the group. We had no idea of the profound feelings she was trying to communicate by suggesting that she needed time alone. We still tried to include her in everything we did, but that was not what she wanted.

During our last meeting together, Crystal handed me a small white box. In it was the tiny rock image Rojo and the Rock Rollers had fashioned for her. She placed the rusty red-and-white stone in my hand. Upon it, as if engraved, was the clear picture of a hawk soaring. "You will receive more from this than I will," she said. "Thank the others for everything we've shared, and when you hold this in your hand, remember me." The words stung. This was a final goodbye to the precious person whom we'd known for years, a delightful lady whose graciousness we all treasured and whose sweet smile we would continue to miss.

It was difficult for us to let Crystal go, but we each knew her choice, no matter how trying, had been made. It was one of the most difficult tests we were asked to accept by the spirit of Sedona. To be able to completely let go of any attachment…even to a dear one…with understanding and love.

* * *

After Rhyan's birth, the ladies and I became armchair travelers, channeling a multitude of beings. Frankly, I began to feel like the counter at 31 Flavors. "Just take a number, please, and wait your turn."

One of the beings who kept asking to come through was Anwar Sadat. He had announced himself over and over again.

A head of state? I don't think so. I wasn't sure I could handle such diversity of information. What a smorgasbord I was receiving—from a rock, to Elvis Presley, to Anwar Sadat. Did I have time for all this? I politely declined again and again until...

It was a gorgeous day in Carmel and the children were riding with me in the car. A nice day for a drive around the ocean, I thought to myself. Rhyan was still quite small and Ian was eagerly begging for a wet suit, over and over again, reminding me of the persistence of Mr. Sadat.

I couldn't help but notice the bright orange GARAGE SALE sign as I turned a corner. Something in my mind shouted, "STOP!" I chided myself about spending money, not to mention time, on things I wouldn't need anyway. "GO ON!" my inner voice pleaded.

Oh, all right. Looking never hurt anyone, I countered. I commandeered Ian to watch Rhyan while I convinced him I'd only be a second or two. Hopping out of the car, I noticed this was not just a typical garage sale. It was more like a small version of Christies. There was so much Limoges and Gucci there my wallet began to tremble right in my hand.

Why had I stopped here? I couldn't even afford the garage-sale prices for these upscale items. This was akin to a chic boutique. You know the kind...nothing is marked, and if you have to ask, you can't afford it.

Just then I spotted it, or, I should say, it found me. As if compelled by an unseen force, I darted to the object on the table, immediately picked it up, handed it to the lady, and asked the price. She looked at it as if it were a foreign object and, holding it high above her head, yelled to her daughter who was climbing the stairs. "How much do you want for this?"

"Oh," and then a long pause..."seven dollars," she replied.

Seven dollars? Nothing here was less than thirty! "I'll take it," I screamed back. Hurriedly, I gave her the money, fearing she'd admit to having made a mistake. Maybe she had really meant seventy!

The lady wrapped the treasure in a brown paper bag before I had barely looked at my bargain. After she handed it to me, I rushed to the car to make my getaway. Safe inside, I carefully unwrapped the finely sculptured, yellow alabaster statuette of Nefertiti. She was beautiful! Eagerly I checked the bottom for some sort of mark. I couldn't believe my eyes! There, taped to the stone was a "calling card of state." The name on the card read…Anwar Sadat. Needless to say, the universe's nudge prompted an acceptance of his invitation to channel him the very next day.

* * *

Anwar Sadat

Good evening to all of you whom I will address as heads of state, for you truly are more dimensional than you realize. It is I, Anwar, who have come this evening, finally, to be able to grant the ability to create peace throughout not only your Earth and our world, but throughout the universe as well. I come to initiate you as emissaries to unite together those who are of the highest caliber of light.

I lived my life knowing that my end days were coming, and that I would be in a place and time where I could not, nor should not, change anything about my circumstances.

As I lay dying, my body riddled with bullets, I could hear the yelling and shouting for only a moment. I could not feel the pain, but I could feel pressure. This pressure is the feeling of betrayal from those who are closest to you. It is most hurtful, more so than any physical pain. No one is deserving of this. It is like being thrown in the middle of the Sahara without a camel, water, or a compass.

I am now considered a diplomat for the entire world. At first I thought, This is impossible. How can I support the world? Then the great Horus spoke to me in a vision and told me to let my heart sweep across the surface of the Earth. This is all that was required. When I heard it, I smiled. How simple. How gracious. How complete.

You are the ambassadors of the world. My heart runs across all of your hearts. Let your souls rise to the extension of the love that you are.

Farewell, my cherished ones.

Second Trip

6

The Love of All Creation

"Good evening, everyone. This is your friend, Rojo. It seems like only yesterday that you walked among us in Sedona, even though two years have passed, and now is the time for you to come again.

"It's been very exciting since you left because you gave us the ability to communicate fully in sentence and structure form with species of life beyond what we felt we knew. Many people come to our area of Arizona to be in the presence of the rocks, but they do not acknowledge us as being a consciousness unto ourselves.

"Wherever you go on the planet, if there is anything you want to know, all you have to do is ask a rock for its encoded information. We are recorders of the beginning of the Earth and the solar system. We are usually millions, if not billions, of years old. You can ask us about every civilization that has gone on from the beginning of time.

"In my home place of Sedona, there's been a great influx of extraterrestrial communication. It would bring me great joy if you would return for a very special event being presented by the Federation, a group of interdimensional, extraterrestrial, and Earth-based beings. They have the ability to heal and have chosen to concern themselves with the Earth's outcome."

* * *

I knew that accepting Rojo's kind invitation was of utmost importance even though a trip to Sedona wouldn't be as easy to swing this time. However, as fate would have it, four of us were able to participate in the celestial celebration.

Sally had located a new place for us to stay close to the Coffee Pot and Steamboat rocks. Perched high on a bluff, we took in excellent views of the surrounding mountains, yet felt secluded from the eyes of the world. We unpacked our bags and made ourselves at home. It was different this time; we had been here before and knew our way around.

When we started channeling that first evening, we met Maja, Rojo's helper. She informed us that he was busy getting everything ready for the Federation event and introduced us to a welcoming committee of coyotes, Whiskey and Lobo, who greeted us from a distance with unexpected enthusiasm.

*   *   *

Maja

Welcome, this is Maja, Rojo's helper. There is much preparation going on for the big celebration tomorrow and great delight in the air. The whole universe is at work expanding souls and touching minds.

AWOooooo.

That's Whiskey you hear. He's welcoming all of you, so do not be afraid. He usually sings only to the moon, but since there is no moon out this evening, he sings for you.

AWOooooo.

He and the dogs you will meet on this trip are akin to the Dog Star, Sirius. Whiskey's been in many lifetimes with each of you. He was known during Egyptian times as the jackal, but he has since elevated himself to be a peace lover. Whiskey, tell them of yourself. They will listen.

AWOooooo.

Remind them of the time you were with them in their Egyptian journeys. [Silence.] It's nothing to be ashamed of, being a jackal.

AWOooooo.

Many other creatures will be coming close to you on your visit here. Do not be afraid, for they only want to see the light beings that have traveled from so far away.

The master hierarchy that reigns throughout the universe has also invited the Star People. It is an exceptional time of creation for all dwellers of the Earth, sky, and rocks; even the rocks of Heaven are uniting once again with the rocks of Earth. And now his friend, Lobo, is joining Whiskey. They will sing to you in harmony.

[Howling in harmony.]

Whiskey has been very suspicious of humans for they have treated him unkindly. Therefore, you should feel honored that he and Lobo are greeting you.

AWOooooo.

There's not much more that I can tell you about the great preparation. Only that by being here, you, too, are a part of the oneness...the opening of all souls and hearts of the planets. Rojo has asked the Cloud People to come closer to create shade for you, and we are planning a great windstorm in your honor. These are the things we can do to let you know you are indeed part of this great occasion. Rojo has been telling us that we are all one and must treat you as we treat ourselves.

I must go now and help to prepare for the celebration of all light beings. I'll leave Whiskey and Lobo to keep you company. They would like you to tone with them now in their key.

[All: Howling in harmony.]

They are most impressed with the voices and the ease with which you did something that other human beings would consider foolishness. Because of your faith and trust in us, you will now be called the 'Two-footed Coyotes.'

*   *   *

The next day, although we had other plans, my guidance had something else in mind. Rojo had led us to many places in Sedona, but this time I felt the spirit of our Native American friend, Running Blue Bear, join him.

"There is a place, close to a famous resort, that you must find. Near there lie the spirits of the 'captured ones,' those who are bound to the Earth forever. Can you help them?" Rojo asked.

This is heavy-duty material we're working on here, I answered silently to the messengers. It seemed we were headed in the wrong direction. I thought we were supposed to hunt for the inverted vortex. But then, as if cued by an inner calling, a hawk soared in front of the car.

"STOP! LOOK!" I gasped, while Sally pulled to the side of the road. "We've got to follow the hawk. Turn around. It will direct us to where we need to go." Sally spun the car around and we found ourselves on a dirt road leading to a resort.

"Healing is why you have come here," Rojo's voice reminded. You will be gifted with feathers from the Great Spirit for making your way to the twisted trees."

I felt this must be important, and if the four of us could help in any way, we certainly would. We noticed the guard posts, the gates, and the massive condominium sitting against the backdrop of the magnificent red canyon. The energy had changed completely. It's difficult to explain a drop in energy…it can only be felt.

"Shhhhh…this is the spot. Park here and we'll walk the rest of the way." I could feel the enthusiasm in Rojo's and Running Blue Bear's vibrations. We passed hedges and rocks as we began to feel our way around. "We must go higher…just a little bit." We headed upward. The foliage was now different, covering the terrain like an eerie, twisted graveyard. The trees here were very old…possibly ancient. The directions came again, loud and clear.

"We must each choose a tree and pray for the spirits of the Indians who are trapped in it," I explained to the others. "Just speak to the tree as if it were a person, because it's holding a displaced soul."

I chose a tree I felt drawn to and, standing before it, began to ask for the release of the soul guarding this sacred site, allowing it to return to its place of origin in the universe. Sally was the last to finish and too far away for us to warn her of approaching hikers on their way up. We stood as if mutes, watching a curious trekker try to find out exactly whom she was speaking to. Immersed in her prayers, chanting and pointing to the heavens, Sally was oblivious of his presence until she received a deep resonant chuckle from the confused gentleman.

"Are you okay?"

Startled and embarrassed, she suddenly realized how she must look having such an animated conversation with a barren, shriveled skeleton of a tree. After trying to convince him of her sanity—only to make matters worse—she joined the stranger in a good, hearty laugh.

Soon, we all felt the energy change. It was somehow lighter and more peaceful after our good deeds. If more people would talk to nature, perhaps the planet could heal in ways now seemingly unknown to us.

The picnic tables and shade at the end of the canyon looked inviting. We had packed a lunch just in case we might spend the day out among the rocks. Nurtured by the coolness of the trees, we took time to relax and discuss what had just taken place. "Hey ho, hey ah, hey ho, hey ah," the words kept running through my mind. "Give thanks for everything," the rock voice chanted along with the deep bass of Running Blue Bear. "It's in the little things of your world that you'll find your true voice. You believe you have done such a small thing, but think again. Together our spirits mediate between the worlds.

"The inch-high people, Kakaka-Kachina of the Hopi, still live in the sacred places. They keep watch over everyone. Look down at your feet and collect a gift from the spirits of Thunder Canyon. They leave these small gray feathers in special thanks to you. May your own spirits always be as light as the feather. Ho."

* * *

Later that afternoon we visited Airport Mesa, one of the highest spots in Sedona. As we passed the lower vortex and traveled to the top of the hill, we could see Thunder Mountain. People claim that large spaceships come and go from this sugarloaf-shaped summit without being noticed. From our viewpoint by the Masonic Temple, looking directly to the north, we paused to search for the Emerald City. Also known as the City of Light, many had described it as casting a green glow at dusk.

If you gaze at this etheric phenomenon long enough, it seems to appear and disappear. It's interesting, also, to watch how clouds in the area form and dissipate even on a clear day. They can exist and then dissolve within moments.

The junipers on Airport Mesa are beautiful with the largest berries I've ever seen. One of the oldest of trees, they are able to absorb negativity and transform it to positive energy. Birds, insects, and small woodland creatures are aware of the safety offered by juniper bushes. In Italy, the juniper is revered because, according to legend, it saved the life of Mary and the infant Jesus when they fled from Herod's assassins. In order to protect her son, she is said to have hidden him beneath a juniper bush.

Rojo asked us to pick the sacred berries and transport them throughout Sedona until we could put them into Oak Creek. By doing so, we would be letting go of anything we no longer wanted to carry for others or ourselves in this lifetime.

There is also a huge cross on this site. After dark, you can always tell where the airport is by the magnificent symbol that lights up the sky. One night on our way home, we noticed a golden streak pass over it as if to say, "Let the light lead your way. Make a wish."

"I wish to see spaceships," Patricia whispered with a touch of whimsy.

"So it shall be," said the little rock voice. "So it shall be."

* * *

That evening after a hurried meal, we headed up Schnebley Road to catch the meteor showers predicted by the news…and so did everyone else. It was super crowded everywhere. This wasn't any fun, so we decided to drive home where we retreated to the glassed-in porch to commune with our spirit friends.

Flickering candles cozily illumined our room. We took familiar places on the comfortable couch, alert to the arrival of any visitors. The waiting intensified as the ceiling made cracking noises and the walls seemed to call out our names. Suddenly, a beam of light penetrated my psyche announcing the Federation's promise. It was time! Time to see the spaceships!

Standing together in the darkness facing the star-lit mountains, we seemed to hover magically out in space. Slowly, a hundred bright dots took their positions above the peaks ahead. While the huge, full moon crept into the velvety blackness, the sparkling points proceeded to bob up and down...back and forth along the silhouette of the mountain range. "Closer," I kept urging. "Just a little closer!"

The minutes ticked by and I was beginning to question the Federation's promise. Without warning, a large triangular ship maneuvered toward us, its green, blue, amber, and red lights sending shivers through my spine. My heart raced, my knees buckled, and I could hardly breathe. All I could hear was an unfamiliar hum and the pounding of my heart.

Sally and Jeanette, squealing with delight, grabbed each other and danced with glee as they witnessed the extraordinary event; but where was Patricia? She had been here just a minute ago. I'd seen my share of spaceships but she hadn't.

"Patricia, where are you? You're missing it," I screamed. "I'm in here," she yelled.

Naturally, at this once-in-a-lifetime event, she was in the bathroom. I hurriedly pulled her out to glimpse the last golden glimmer of the awesome object passing over our heads.

When we finally calmed down, we were limp but exhilarated and grateful for having experienced such a spiritual event. We felt united with all creation. Even the dogs, who had spent most of the evening yelping, were now hauntingly quiet.

* * *

Settling in for a late-night channeling after all the commotion and holding the juniper berries in our hands, we were graced by the loving presence of Mother Mary. Slowly, she began to speak through me:

Mother Mary

I am Mary, mother to the Christ in all of you. Thank you for allowing my Son to enter your lives. We have waited centuries for you to receive the love of all creation. It was the calling from your hearts that got the attention of the Federation, the Ascended Masters, my Son, and this little rock. We want to tell you this, for it is the orchestration of your lives that creates the pattern in which outward events take place. You are always in the kingdom of the Creative Light.

I leave you with the blessings of my Son and my spirit. May you always walk with the Masters. Let me now share with you this prayer.

Prayer to Creation

Beloved one who is within us,
we come forward each day to be in the Light
of the universe of Love in all of its glory.
Lead us not into the realms of thinking
that are limited or not progressive,
for it is the soul that lights the universe
and the stars beyond.
Grant us this Light and forgive us every thought
that is of limited consciousness,
for we are one with all the forms of Light.
Within the expression of The All,
each of us is created unto the other
with Power and Love forever, and ever, and ever.
Amen. Amen. Amen.

This was the first time I had contacted Mary's soft, yet powerful energy. When I came out of trance and began to notice what was happening, I was astounded to see the ladies kneeling around me, crying and holding onto my hands and feet. This jarred me from a still-heavy alpha state. So intense was the feeling of another world that I couldn't tell if I was alive or dead. I wondered if I had gone too far out of my body.

"Did I die? Am I alive?" These were the first audible words I could issue in my own voice.

The ladies, doubled up with laughter at the picture of themselves fawning over a mere mortal, assured me that I was definitely still among the living.

7

Farewell for Now

It was late afternoon before we returned to the rocks of Sedona. Regretting we hadn't arrived sooner, we scampered down to "frog rock," reliving with joy our last visit there. Off came our shoes and socks to let hot feet sink into the cool spring water. Soon we remembered the juniper berries and tossed them into the stream along with heartfelt wishes. As I soaked in the sun, the lapping of the water became the voice of Oak Creek, acknowledging our wishes and reminding us of its existence.

Oak Creek

I am the waters and the streams, the form of liquid in your life. I am movement...I am life. I am Oak Creek that runs throughout this area. At times I flow in great steady processes but sometimes I merely trickle. My existence becomes, and then unbecomes, in order to feel the presence of the beings that hold themselves in the form of rocks, manzanita, trees, animals, and insects. It is an honor to be a creek, a lake, or even a mud puddle...for there is energy in all things.

The tears from your eyes come from the eyes of God. The rain that falls into my vast crevices also comes from God. There is nothing more wonderful than discovering the true ability of knowing yourself—no matter what you are, whether a human, bird, rock, or a creek. We are all the same, for we all have the energy of the Creator, of the Father/Mother, of the life that streams in and out of every day and every night.

I suppose you would consider me an elder for I have seen the mountains and people come and go. I have seen the sky change and felt the breeze and the heat of the sun. I have felt the warmth of those who have touched me, and I know of their desire to heal, to love, and to play. I am one with the Earth, nor can I ever be separated from it. I see the stars, the sky, the sun, and the moon...the beauty in everything.

People of the Earth, strive to flow like a river or creek and be one with all of your surroundings. As the great changes take place you will know. As the great sun in its heat trades places with the moon, you will know. Like the vastness of the land and the greatness of the sea, you shall know, too, how great you are.

* * *

We reverently contemplated the words of Oak Creek, barely aware that the sun had set. It was difficult to rejoin the real world...the world of shoes and socks, and finding our way back without a flashlight. But somehow we didn't seem to care. The bliss was still there. Castle Rock was a'hum with the channels of light.

This is the place to come to traverse time, space, and maybe even a dimension or two. Don't be surprised if you hear the song of angels in the river. "Beauty is everywhere," Rojo's little voice chimed in. "Just like the smile of God, it casts itself upon all things."

* * *

It was our last evening in Sedona, and we piled onto the couches in the living room to connect with Rojo once more before leaving.

"I am here. It is me, Rojo. We're missing you already, and you haven't even gone yet. We had such a wonderful time watching you out amongst the living creatures of the forest: the lizards in Boynton Canyon and the little flying creatures that go 'rippetee, rippetee, rippetee.' We also sent two butterflies, scheduled to come later in the season but who volunteered to be with you. The big, black bumblebee, though, couldn't understand why you screamed and ran away when it buzzed so close. It just wanted to see the new visitors.

"The Cloud People are very sad you are leaving. Not everyone looks forward to Cloud People because they predispose rain. But what many turn away, you've invited as part of your existence when you're here. They feel very honored to be accepted.

"Like-minded consciousness runs through all life. Oak Creek asked you to put your vibrational field into the water spirits. Your energy will now travel to Arizona, New Mexico, California, and even Mexico simply because you got your feet wet. Much more than that has happened, however. You have invited other consciousnesses to come through. You also greeted the waters at the dry lake bed and the stagnant pool. We wanted you to see that without a flow through all forms, the energy becomes spoiled.

"Many different times Sally noticed squirrels with their mouths filled with nuts. These animal spirits wished to guide you on your journey. The great hawk also chose to guide you, but only from a distance. The squirrels gave signals to each other—when to cross in front of your car. There was one doubter squirrel, however, that very narrowly escaped. Fortunately, Sally saw him and saved his life, so there will be a time when he will save her life, too. Nothing goes unnoticed in the consciousness of living embodiment which desires only peace, harmony, and love throughout the world.

"We, combined, have done so much to join our consciousnesses in order to bridge the worlds between us. We will miss you greatly until our hearts meet again.

"Goodbye for now, with fondness and love.

"Your rock friends."

* * *

Once again it was time to catch our plane home from Sedona. Our trip had been much too short, and we couldn't believe our magical time together was at an end. Or was it?

8

Out of This World

I'd been ignoring the wake-up messages in the middle of the night informing me our mission wasn't yet finished. But the physical signals—high-pitched noises and clicking sensations within the bridge of my nose—were hard to ignore. It was more and more evident that the Federation was contacting me...loudly and clearly.

"Your journeys are not complete. Now that you have committed yourselves to the discovery of our combined work on this planet, there's more still to come."

I had always been subconsciously aware of the Federation's participation in my life, but now I was fully awake to its existence. The contact with them triggered the memory of my first UFO encounter and reminded me that we are not alone in this universe. The term universe contains the parts uni ("one") and versus ("to turn"). The roots of this word imply that we are "turned into one" within the magnificence of all life.

* * *

The first experience I ever remember of a contact occurred when I was nine. I awoke abruptly in the middle of the night, drawn in and transfixed by a light emanating from my bedroom window. Red, yellow, blue, and green flashes circled in a rhythmic pattern outside while I made an effort to focus more clearly. I saw that the lights were mounted on a small, saucer-shaped metal craft. By the time my mind had figured out what it was observing, I had jumped back into bed, pulling the covers up over my head.

Later that night, I awakened to the gush of blood flowing down my throat. Half asleep, I forced myself to sit up. Alarmed by my red-stained pillow, I called to my parents who were visibly shaken by what they saw. After an ice pack and about 10 minutes of trying to stop the bleeding, I insisted they accompany me outside. There on the front lawn, my father, armed with his flashlight, discovered a 12"-wide band 6' in diameter, burned into the grass. It was a perfect circle. It was reassuring to know I wasn't the only one who had observed this occurrence.

*   *   *

Many years later, a UFO again visited me, this time much larger. It was while I was living in Muk Chong Dong, Osan Air Base, Korea, with my husband, Michael. We had been married only a few weeks when permission was granted by the Air Force for me to accompany him. Generally, wives could not go with airmen to their assignments at Osan, so this meant we would have to live off base. The Air Force made it clear they would not be able to insure my safety in any way. I was on my own as far as behavior and liability were concerned. I was definitely filled with apprehension, being a young lady of twenty-one on an adventure in a foreign country. This was partly because Michael worked twenty-four hour shifts. It was during one such shift that my close encounter took place.

One evening, as on many others, I went to the fire station carrying Michael's dinner. As usual, I stayed until the 10:00 p.m. curfew. Whenever I was there that late, I had to catch a ride on the Kim Chee bus to the main gate and then proceed to walk three blocks to our compound…alone. This night was like any other, except that I had waited a little too long to make my way home. I took the final bus and was one of two people on the vehicle. The gate also was quiet, desolate except for the MP in the little booth.

Muk Chong Dong is a little town, even by Korean standards. It is laid out like an old-west ghost town, and on this night it truly resembled one. Everything seemed particularly still and all the shops, bustling and busy in the daytime, were closed tight. Even the constant night life of topless bars and the usual flow of taxis was not evident. Then I remembered. It was a religious holiday and people were in full compliance with the occasion.

As I stepped off the bus, a strange feeling came over me...a feeling of being watched. I searched the street in front of me, scoured the road behind, and checked out the bushes. Nothing. Yet, I felt the presence of unseen eyes...watching and waiting. It was an uneasy sensation. Then, as if in slow motion, I looked up into the sky. Above me, in the moonless dark, I saw something. Brown against the black sky and the length of a football field, it loomed. I spotted porthole-shaped openings along its circumference, and then I became aware of something else. The stark silence! I couldn't believe that such a huge craft could be so quiet.

Fear gripped me and my knees literally began to shake, an experience I had never before felt in such a physical way. It was imperative that I make it home quickly. I took off running, thinking, I'm not going with you this time. Not now. Not...ever. It seemed like an eternity to run those three short blocks. I fumbled for my key to the barbed-wire gate and hastily entered the compound. Too terrified to glance skyward, I locked myself in the tiny room, grabbed the sheets, covered my head, and wished for Michael so I wouldn't be alone.

Missing time! I have no recollection of what happened that night...or the next day. I only know *they* knew when and where to find me...anywhere on Earth.

Through the ensuing years, these experiences never left my conscious mind. I knew there were beings who could affect my life, but I wouldn't let thoughts of what might happen overtake me. Every now and then a communication would make itself known, but I never got used to the connection. Nevertheless, I was constantly drawn to the metaphysical and my curiosity continued to push me to find out more. Until now, *they* had been very quiet, even though meanwhile I had seen many crafts. Nevertheless, it wasn't until I returned from Korea that verbal contact would be made.

* * *

Some friends invited me to a seance in Los Angeles, home to all kinds of paranormal wonder in more ways than one. It sounded interesting and exciting, yet I had always been a tad leery of seances since viewing the silly Hollywood film versions. After some coaxing, however, I agreed that it might be fun.

When we arrived at the building on Beverly Boulevard, I noticed twenty, maybe thirty people waiting at the door. They all looked pretty normal to me. This might be okay, I convinced myself. Joining the line, I knew it would be only moments until the door opened. The entrance was jammed with spirit seekers, candles, and crystals. We waited there a few minutes before making our way into a larger room encircled with aluminum folding chairs. Eagerly we found our seats—mine was directly across from the medium. Between us, in the middle of the circle, stood a single chair. On it sat an 8"x10" pastel drawing of a bald, translucent-skinned man in a high-neck, uniform-like jacket. His eyes were the palest blue I had ever seen. I couldn't stop looking at him.

Once the lights were dimmed, the medium took her seat. She began by channeling Abraham Lincoln and then Thomas Jefferson. When she had finished with both of them, she asked the group, "Is there a Rosemary in the room?"

A little unnerved, I thought surely there must be someone else here with my name! No one responded. A bit impatiently the question was asked again. Drat. This could go on all night. "Yes," I forced the word out of my mouth.

"I have a message for you," the medium replied. "It's from the being in the picture in front of you. Do you recognize him?" "Who, me? Him? Well, kind of…, I mean, I was drawn to him." Okay! I couldn't take my eyes off of him, my inner thoughts jolted. "Yes, I think so," I voiced timidly.

"This is Commander Uri. He invites you to join him on his spaceship tonight. He wants to take you for a ride!"

A RIDE! Great. That's just what I needed to hear! Swallowing hard, I sputtered and squeaked, "Me??"

"Yes, and dress warmly, for you will be traveling to a distant galaxy and you must protect your body for the long journey."

I glanced at the people around me. Many sat gawking with their mouths half open, while others looked enviously at my nodding response to the invitation. "Heh, heh," I laughed nervously, trying to brush off the whole episode.

The seance had ended. My friends were delighted for me. The idea of a ride in a spaceship thrilled them. "Good. Let's trade places. I'll give my ride away," I offered.

"Oh, no. Have fun with it," my friend smiled.

Later that night, I thought, Yeah, this is some fun...lying here awake all night dressed in these long johns I haven't had occasion to use since I left Korea. Hour after hour passed as I watched the ceiling. I was just begging Commander Uri to reconsider when a loud explosion boomed outside my window.

This is it, my mind shrieked. Holding my hands over my eyes, I peeked between my fingers to check the time. Suddenly, it was dark everywhere...even the streetlights had gone out. There was no electricity anywhere except for my digital clock. This was eerie! Shaking, I stared at the blinking green numbers. 3:33 A.M. it flashed. I ran to the window and saw what looked like the Fourth of July. Sparks of all colors spouted and flew, but I couldn't make out what was happening. Hysterically, I grabbed the telephone and called my friend. "They're here! They're coming to get me!"

"Calm down," she insisted. "If they had come to get you, you'd be gone by now."

Her words made sense, but maybe...maybe they miscalculated and hit the transformer instead. God, how I hoped so.

Deja vu was now in full force. Did I really take a ride that night or had I been saved by an error in a longitudinal miscalculation? The answers were inside me somewhere. One day I might find out.

* * *

On December 31st that same year, I was invited by a friend to a New Year's Eve party. She was the only person I knew there, and everyone else was playing with the Ouiji Board. As I went over to join in, the people on the board received a message.

"Rosemary, there's a message for you." How nice, I thought, a message for me. "The board is spelling it now. It's from U...R...I. It just keeps spelling U...R...I. Will you accept the message?"

"No! I don't think so," I replied hastily.

Why, I didn't know. All I knew was I wasn't ready anytime soon for another spaceship ride. I understood the Universal Law that states no extra-terrestrial being can take you without your permission. Each person has free will. This "will" applies to an agreement...the Creator's agreement. People who have mentioned their abductions to me sometimes question this statement, but I remind them that will has both a conscious and a subconscious element to it. Even though consciously you may be saying no, your subconscious mind might already have given permission. If you have been abducted, a part of you consented, either in this lifetime or in another, to allow the contact to be made. Perhaps you still are linked genetically to these beings, thereby allowing communication of some kind to take place. Whatever the terms of the past, the Universal Law can always be reapplied, if needed. Commander Uri respected my wishes, but who knows what lies in store for the future.

Third Trip

9

Devil's Bridge

Destiny and the constant call to again visit Sedona became too difficult to ignore. Because our work with many sincere beings was uppermost in our minds, we were committed to go there a third time to complete our mission. Although it wasn't easy to plan the itinerary due to Jeanette's last-minute cancellation and the resulting chaos, the remaining three of us ultimately made the connection with Sedona.

This time we stayed in a quaint, rustic lodge on the opposite side of town. Set off by itself, it afforded privacy for our nightly escapades into the world of channeling. There we would meet a Bengal tiger, a Masai warrior, an Anasazi chief, and many others who helped direct our true purpose.

In the still of the evening after settling in, Rojo's friendly voice opened our hearts.

"It is I, Rojo, welcoming you to Sedona once again. We're very happy you are here. It seems like so many things were trying to distract you that we wondered if you would actually be able to come.

"It's a small example of how life is going to be in the future...many decisions and departures from original plans. So far you are adjusting well, allowing the higher powers of being to take their natural course. You've passed a very good test.

"Many unexpected things will be happening to you on this trip…all positive, of course, but slightly different from what you're used to. Even your plans have shown great diversity, yet you've taken the 'bull by the reins' in order to unite together and be with the energies of Sedona.

"To get here, you had many emotions to overcome, but you persevered in spite of your tears. Even rocks cry, though differently. We do have emotions but are still learning about them as we become more like the humans that surround us.

"We have seen humans come and go, and now many are coming to stay in the Sedona area. We are happy they are here, and our only hope is that they honor our existence. This is our greatest wish, to be able to cohabitate with humans and share harmony all the way around.

"The bright one [Jeanette] is not here. This is part of the process. You, the trinity, are to carry on and go forward in your natural adventures to unite states of consciousness of other beings and entities. You will be led, and you must trust the forces."

* * *

The hike up to Devil's Bridge seemed like a trek we could easily manage. After all, the guidebook stated only .9 of a mile. What it neglected to mention was that the trail climbed steadily uphill the whole way.

We'd gotten a late start, around noonish, and proceeded on our way. I felt the weather get hotter and hotter, though not as hot as it usually would be at this time of the year. I knew Rojo had done everything in his power to cool things off for me. Do I have control over the weather? I wouldn't presume to think so…but when in Sedona, I request cooler weather and it seems to happen that way.

As we started up the trail, I felt my weight pull against me and longed for some shade in which to take a breather. Looking for a place to stop, I glanced down and spied a familiar object. What's this? Another button? Yes, a small, round, dark one. Let's see, on our first trip we were given a white button, and now another one…only brown. The little rock voice let me know this seemingly small, insignificant object was a symbol of our work here. In fact, it was meant as a significant sign about which we were soon to learn more.

The steeper the incline became, the more I slowed. And then, there it was, my refuge. A red-rock inlet, a scoop in the side of the mountain. "Let's sit here," I begged Patricia. "I'll catch my breath and channel some information." I knew she loved the channeling and, bless her heart, she could sense that I needed to rest my bod. It wasn't the optimal place to receive information, with everyone and his brother hiking by, but Rojo's voice kicked in to let me know I was doing the right thing.

Suddenly, I felt the presence of a loving guide named Zeela, Rojo's friend from the City of Light. Before my eyes she projected several clear, luminescent, merkabah vehicles, tetrahedron in formation, floating out in the canyon ahead of us. She urged us to let go of any fear we might have involving life itself. As human beings, we always seem to be working on that subject. In this instance, the fears involved possible hiking hazards, physical limitations and, in my own case, heat stroke.

Fortunately, Sally's enthusiasm never waned. "I'll go up first," she offered cheerfully, "and tell you what it's like."

All too soon, Sally returned. "You've got to see the bridge. It's fabulous! If you don't go, you'll really be missing something." (She also promised us lots of goodies, including a delicious salmon dinner, if we'd just follow her up those steep, precarious steps.)

At that moment, a black-and-white dog, desperately thirsty, made his way down the stone incline looking exhausted. Unfortunately, his owner had left his water in the car. Without hesitation, Sally and Patricia rose to the occasion by pulling an empty licorice box out of the backpack and pouring Evian into the thin, shallow container. The dog eagerly slurped the cool water, thanked us with his beautiful eyes, and trotted merrily on his way.

The Maiden Staircase to Devil's Bridge was awaiting our arrival. It required a nearly vertical ascent up the naturally formed stones if we were to touch a piece of heaven. Crafted against the high mountain by the elements, they issued their challenge.

Why were we hesitant? Even the elderly with bulging backpacks and those afraid of heights were managing quite well.

"Come to the top and experience the wonder of it all," Rojo's voice urged. "It's another earthly place held suspended in time and space." The mysterious invitation resonated in my head.

"It's this way," Sally encouraged. Patricia and I labored up the steep, treacherous steps until we reached a ledge from which we could view the entire canyon. The brilliance of nature's colors and the immensity of it all began to sink in. It seemed that a beautiful Indian blanket had been spread out over the entire landscape.

"Just a little higher," Sally prompted. "This is the last bit." By now we had thrown out all caution and willingly followed her the rest of the way. As we rounded the last step, we grasped the meaning of her persistence. A natural stone bridge, long and vast, jutted out, creating a huge portal below. To see it surrealistically hanging there in space boggled the mind. We felt a distinct invitation emanating from its being, tempting even the most timid. The canyon floor was lost by comparison, leaving one with the sense that the span above truly hung in mid-air.

As Patricia and I surveyed the awesome formation, Sally whisked her way out to the center. Simultaneously, a red-and-white helicopter popped up behind her, validating just how high we really were. "Come on out here," Sally shouted.

Patricia and I looked intently at each other as if needing more reason to complete this final test. We briefly reiterated the positives: "We're already here…we've come all this way…what a shame it would be not to. Let's do it!"

The decision had been made but, like children making a pact, we pinky swore to do it together. Arm in arm, we led ourselves out a wee bit more. Step by step, we edged onto the bridge, hanging recklessly above the whole world. With eyes partially closed and hearts pounding, we shuffled forward, half-expecting to fall off at any moment. When we finally reached the middle, we looked at each other in total surprise. Hey, that wasn't half as scary as we had imagined. In fact, there was plenty of stone to stand on. Together we laughed and gave each other a giant hug, celebrating our accomplishment.

"Fear is an illusion," the little voice chimed in. "It appears to be something it isn't, just like the Devil's Bridge."

Yes, I silently agreed. We had conquered the bridge that seemed so narrow and dangerous. It turned out that the gape below was formidable only from the approach. When we had the courage to follow through, the journey proved natural and effortless.

Rojo's message was certainly clear: "Love is a portal that bridges the worlds of fear and faith. Sometimes life is like the Devil's Bridge, projecting negativity onto the road ahead; yet when it is lived with confidence, endurance, and trust, our existence becomes instead a Rainbow Bridge, connecting to All That Is."

* * *

Zeela

This is Zeela, your guide from the City of Light. By accomplishing your task today upon the bridge, you have been rewarded with an elevation of light consciousness. Sally caught on quickly and the two of you took your time, but it doesn't matter who was first or last. What matters is that you combined your skills to create not separation, but completeness. This is the way the great Masters on the other side have hoped everyone will work out their fears and disbeliefs; and if it can be done with only three, it can be done with the multitudes as well.

Where light is, happiness exists. Light exists in many forms—healing, laughter, love, and kindness—which all dispel fear. That is what you did today...conquer fear by facing difficulties with an open heart and the assurance of safety. The light was there to guide each of you on your chosen path. The devil is but a trickster who plays mind games through fear. That's why we like to call this place Angel's Hollow instead of Devil's Bridge, for beneath the darkness lies a firm stronghold of love.

I would like to tell you more about the City of Light and why you are here. This realm does exist and will be reflected to you many times while on your journey. We have programmed your brain cells with a frequency to help you become aware of sacred geometrical shapes comprising the etheric planes.

From this day forward your Merkabahs are fully activated and constantly protecting you. They create an energy grid to safeguard all your bodies—physical, emotional, mental, spiritual, and cosmic. The Great Brotherhood is issuing them now to the light workers because many protection techniques, like using shields and bubbles of light, may not be enough. The Merkabah is a much more refined process and is necessary for the coming times.

Remember when you saw the City of Light that day on Airport Mesa? It is actually more of a family than a city, and its countless members dwell in the consciousness of the Most High, surrounded by the Great Brotherhood and the Masters. You can go there if you are ever feeling alone.

When you visualize this beautiful city, it will indeed encapsulate you in the most brilliant of frequencies. It belongs to all of those beings, human and non, who choose to graduate at the highest level of their existence and go forward on the path of light.

There was a gentleman who watched everything you did today as if it were a great story he intended to be part of. This elder with a gnarled staff is a kind and brave person whose years have not stopped him from facing new challenges. That is the same for you, Patricia. The two of you became kindred spirits the moment you bravely forged the trail together. Both of you are enthusiastic about life and have a deep understanding of nature. You not only stood close to each other, but your spirits danced in the heavens. You were showing each other that if one can do it, the other can too, no matter what the chronological age.

This is a great breakthrough, for in the City of Light there is no age. It's the love and courage of spirit that make our people who they are. It's that enthusiasm to try, to go forward...the sense of non-limitation. This is what the City of Light is trying to teach. This, in essence, is true living.

The initiations you are taking with the help of the Great Brotherhood and Ascended Masters—along with the angels who guided your ascent up the sandstone steps towards heaven—are bringing you closer and closer to what God is. More and more often you are trusting that all is well...always. Knowing this is your safety.

When Jesus turned the water into wine, it was the nature of his doing so that changed things. Each of you who is listening to the higher forces has come from your heart and soul to reunite dimensions and heal the rips that others may have caused. As an example, the dog who needed the water was doubtful he could go on, but you miraculously manifested water...like Jesus. At least that's what your Sirian dog-friend thought.

And so I shall leave you with tears of understanding and joy, for every day in your lives is a miracle. The City of Light is always there to replenish your hopes, wishes, and dreams. It will remind you of the preciousness of life here on this earthly sphere.

For you who walk without wings, can also fly.

* * *

"Hi, it's Rojo checking in. Did you enjoy your day today? We were all watching you hike up to the Sacred Bridge and were laughing to see Rosemary complain the whole way. We liked it when you put the water down her neck to cool her off, Sally. That was very funny.

"When you come to Sedona, you restore the faith of all the rocks...that there are people who care and who listen. You have come because of your love for us. You are truly Rock People, too.

"We have heard you pray from the heart, 'Dear God, help the Rock People and the Hopi lands. Help the environment to be free, clear, and clean. Help it to have water and the perfect balance of nature.'

"Everybody should do this. Whenever they step out of their homes onto their land, they should bless it in the same way. It would create a unified field of understanding to preserve the preciousness of the Earth.

"Because you have come, the rocks of the whole universe are singing 'Home, home on the range.' Mr. Wilson, the prospector whose name you saw on the plaque today, taught us that song in the 1890s. He was well known in this area as a big, brave bear-hunter man. He was also an alcoholic, and some of his stories were quite far-fetched. But he was a nice being...very much of a loner. He would sing to himself in the evening, 'Home, home on the range,' and all the little rocks would gather around him. It was wonderful there under the stars…until, of course, he passed out.

"I must leave now. I have to help with the weather. It may be very hot tomorrow if I don't get going."

10

The City of Light

Sally was always the first one up, ready to face the day with a brisk walk. This morning she had plotted a course to check out the nearby area.

Enjoying the crisp morning air, she happened upon a crystal shop that was advertising a big sale. To her surprise, however, the premises were devoid of any activity. Parked in the driveway was a well-worn older-model Chevy van. Dented and rusted, it definitely looked out of place. As she inched closer to the door of the shop, she was startled by a loud "PSSSST!" Alarmed, she spun around.

"Come here. Ya wanna see somethin'?" A gruff, muffled voice almost commanded. Perceiving waves of acrid smoke billow from the window of the van, Sally hesitated.

"Excuse me, are you speaking to me?" Instead of an answer, Sally met a shadowy figure leaping from the van. The shirtless and scantily over-alled Jethro-like stranger smiled a toothy grin.

"Yep. It's the biggest thang you'll ever see!" He was confident, even jubilant. Not knowing what he had in mind, Sally began asking her angels to surround and protect her.

"It's around the back. Come on over here and I'll show it to ya." Her mind still reeling with apprehension, she cautiously followed him to the rear of the van. Suddenly, without warning, he flung open the double doors and suspiciously removed a dark tarp from the floor of the vehicle. Still praying, Sally held her breath and bravely peeked into the open cavity.

"Isn't it the biggest thang you've ever seen?" the colorful stranger inquired.

"Gosh, yes," was her relieved reply. "How did you ever get it in there?"

"It broke my axle in Oklahoma, it's so darn heavy...'bout 1500 pounds."

"I've never seen one quite that large before." Sally was truly impressed. There in front of her sat a gigantic single piece of quartz crystal in perfect condition. Nestled around it were hundreds more, all of pristine quality.

Just then the front door to the shop opened and a mature, engaging lady appeared. "Come in and see the rest of them. We're having a sale this weekend. This kind man has traveled all the way from Arkansas to share these carefully mined crystals."

Feeling much calmer, Sally willingly accepted and spent the morning intuitively choosing a number of gorgeous specimens to take home.

As she left the shop, she heard a distinctive drawl holler, "You all come back now!"

*   *   *

Later, as we regrouped and began our evening session, Patricia came into her element. Nothing was more exciting to her than channeling all night long.

Zeela

Hello everyone, this is Zeela. The crystals you purchased today are representative of the many facets of the City of Light. The different features of each crystal—the rainbows, pyramids, even the tiny snowflakes and alien ships—are, in essence, of Lemurian or Atlantean origin.

The City of Light that exists in the heavens above was born as a reflection of these societies, for 'as above, so below.' During the past two nights, your etheric presence has explored the City of Light in the 13th dimen-

sion. You were dressed in the rainbow colors of our beautiful city, shim-
mering and reflecting pink as you mingled among us here.

The beings of our realm no longer have access to human form. Neither
were your etheric bodies connected to a form while you were here; there-
fore, it was easy for us to allow you to come. Let me describe your entrance
into the City of Light so that you may journey along in your mind.

City of Light Visualization

Take a deep breath, relax, and visualize an angel on either side of you.
They invite your etheric body forward and fly you gently and easily to a
corridor of light. As you reach it, they stay behind and guard the entrance
to the City.

Now, make your way safely down into a crystalline structure, a gigantic
hallway of reflective beauty, just as if you were entering a crystal from
the open side. As you go forward, the light radiates in impulses of your
thought processes, and the higher they are, the lighter the tunnel becomes.
As you open your mind to what lies ahead, the corridor becomes lighter
and lighter.

Before you are golden, cathedral-like doors. As you come closer, they
automatically open inward, introducing you to a magnificent city. See the
spectacular entryway lit with fountains, waterfalls, and colorful plants in
every hue you can imagine. Shimmering trees of pink and yellow line the
circular path. You glide along a translucent floor made of a substance
similar to fluorite through which you can see below to the blue sky, the
Earth, and the mountains and valleys that are your lifespring. Ahead of
you is a series of crystalline steps and another platform...a new level of
being. Take those steps upward; and as you do, you go into an exquisite
Milky Way room. In it are 100,000 stars shining and twinkling, just like
the Milky Way at night. Walk down a hallway to where it widens, and
curves, and turns into the next room.

This room is built like the Taj Mahal with fluorescent-blue round
spheres and pointed spirals. The lights and colors are magnificent. We share
these colors with you, for we know you can see them in the trueness of
their being. In this blue room is Mother Mary's very simple chair. It sits

on a raised platform all by itself with the sun's beautiful rays beaming from it. Surrounding her chair are roses in all colors of the rainbow—reds, pinks, blues, purples, magentas, and greens.

Mother Mary is illuminated in this beautiful cavern of light. As she walks down the stairs, she embraces you tenderly and wraps you in a lovely scarf of blue, presenting you with a red, crystalline rose. You relax as she invites you to sit. Please be silent for a moment and listen to what she is telling you.

Mary gently takes both of your hands in hers, gives you a kiss on each cheek, and thanks you for coming, for she knows there's much ahead to do.

She now shows you a large, square, sparkling silver door. As you reach it, it opens inward and you are in yet another room. The Council of Twelve sit at a gigantic crystal table, awaiting your entrance. Throughout the room are enormous mirrors, reflecting the truth within you. The twelve Ascended Masters— Buddha, The Christ, Djwal Khul, El Morya, Hilarion, Kuan Yin, Kuthumi, Maha Chohan, Maitreya, Sanat Kumara, Serapis Bey, and St. Germain—come forward to greet you by taking your hand and introducing themselves, one by one. They bow, acknowledging your presence.

We appreciate it that you have come and we honor your existence. Please, sit at the table and have the sparkling wine and delicious food we have prepared. Ingest them as you do all life's lessons, with anticipation and eagerness. Taste the delicious flavors fully and know that they nourish every part of you.

The Masters want to acknowledge and speak with you. Let those who radiate to you come forward. Take a moment to listen.

Now they show you a brilliant, copper doorway with a pyramid-shaped opening. You may enter into the corridor of opalescence, which reflects the splendor of all the colors surrounding you. Through this triangular corridor, you may see a most beautiful being known to you as Jesus. He comes forward, and around him is a lush garden with flora, fauna, rain-bows, clouds, sky, ocean, flowers, fields of wheat, and running rivers.

It is the Lord Master himself who welcomes you like a father hugging his own children. 'Come sit with me,' he says, and you sit beside him on a shimmering opaline rock. He looks into your faces lovingly and with joy, asking for your ideas about what you think the Earth needs. Take a moment to discuss your thoughts with the Master.

Now he kisses you on your forehead and beckons you to follow him up a spiraling staircase of light. He wants to show you what the world looks like from where he abides. As you reach the threshold surrounding the Master, he waves his hand and the universe opens, revealing the planets and stars in their total splendor. As he speaks, he speaks of all lifeforms everywhere.

The world and the universe are open to you, for those who have faith have everything. For those who have love have the ALL. The universe is waiting. Fly wherever you like. You will be safe. Travel wherever you want, whether it's to a planet, a star system, or back to Earth. Go, I will be waiting. Feel yourself flying through the worlds, the planets, and the stars. Journey through the dimensions if you wish. They are all breathtaking...each and every one.

Allow yourself to be gifted...to be total...to be whole. Be in love with yourself as you *are* in love with the Master. Do not think that it is too vast, that you cannot make a choice. You have all that is open to you...all that exists on every plane. The angels are traveling with you. They comfort you. These are the same beings that brought you through the City of Light this time and shall now return you to your bodies.

As you feel your angels gently guiding you back into this room, know that the City of Light awaits you every evening if you choose. You may visit as often as you like. You are one of us...you *are* us...we are all one. The City of Light grows with your love and attention. We will always be there for you. Simply think of us and we will appear.

11

Conference Calls

We all felt this last trip was an affirmation of the work we'd accomplished so far. It had been magical and would continue to be.

"This time you will meet spirit teachers along your path," Rojo reminded us. "Take time to listen to their words. Look to the truth deep within their souls, and you will see yourselves."

With that in mind, we snuggled into our comfy chairs one evening as, one by one, beings from another time and space began to grace us with their presence.

* * *

Moha

This is Moha, Elder of the Rock People and your spirit guide from Bell Rock. Your journeys have been of great importance, not only to Rojo but also to all the participants in the Federation celebration that your etheric bodies attended. Rojo invited all of the life forms of the dimensions in the universe to meet and participate with you in the Earth's galactic review. The animal spirits of the Earth were also asked to give their opinions and trade knowledge with all, for they are such a large part of existence on Earth.

As you crossed the bridge—the portal between the worlds—all fear was cleared away from you, and your knowledge, understanding, and love of life were reactivated. The force of nature is great, but the mind of man is greater still. With your mind, you can perform all of the miracles that nature teaches and God allows you.

* * *

As Moha's wise words faded into the distance, a solemn, resonant voice echoed from the deep caverns of ancient caves. I could see his brown, soulful eyes reflecting adoration for the land of his people. The desert sky urged him to speak of the inner wisdom he needed to share.

Talocka Chooka

I am Talocka Chooka from the Elder Clan of the Anasazi tribes. I wish to tell you of things to come.

The ancient ways that hold sacred secrets about people and their connection to the stars need to be brought forward, for the time is near for a change. The Kokopelli flute players are calling forward the heavens. The Earth is in jeopardy. The shallow roots of man have spread out and people are no longer able to hold the energy of the planet. The waters, the land, and the rock people of all nations are straining to keep the planet together.

At the conference, you met with Earth's chieftain energies who now live in the heavens. They represent indigenous peoples and animals who claim the Earth as their sacred home.

The landmasses are shifting and must continue to do so, for a stagnant Earth would cause even more upheaval and tribulation. The wind and weather patterns will also change as all life on Earth begins to fade away.

Many brothers and sisters in the animal kingdom are leaving the Earth at this time...going home in their soul essence to their planets of origin.

This will leave your home without animals or the benefit from the jobs they do so well.

Fruit and berries are becoming smaller and vegetables have been contaminated by the hand of man. Because of continual tampering, probing, and spraying of chemicals, the birds and larger animal species are no longer able to eat insects that have tasted the no-longer juicy, luscious fruit.

Man's diseases have taken over and caused fatigue among the species on the Earth. The cats—cougars, tigers, and panthers—are also being afflicted by imbalances caused by humans. All animals on the Earth are losing their energy due to man's undying belief that he, himself, rules all. Without healthy birds and animals, the insect population will flourish and destroy much of the food.

The masterpiece of the Earth can do fine without man. He should act only as a respectful visitor, tending the land and making it livable for other creatures...not merely himself. Unfortunately, because of man's lack of consideration, the chain of existence has been jeopardized. As it begins to rot away, there will be no justice created for him.

I come neither as a herald of doom nor a prophet of destruction, but as an enlightened one to share the knowledge of what is happening. I seek to make you aware of the future so it can be changed.

There is much hope in the Council of the Holy Ones that the Earth and the people on it can renew themselves. Please use this Anasazi prayer to reenact joy and abundance in your daily lives.

The Seeker's Prayer

Givers of knowledge and light,
crystalline structures of love,
visionaries of every hue,
the Great Council has accepted you.
May your hearts go out to everyone.
May you allow the wind to take you
wherever it is you need to go.
Journey across the planet with your feet.

Others will know of your presence.
You will change the land with each step.
You will be kind to each one you meet
and offer them food and drink.
You will heal their souls by walking with them
and taking them where they need to go.
You will remain strong and grow even taller.
You will grow so tall that you will
see each corner of the Earth,
and view each corner of the heavens,
and you will touch the two-leggeds
as you touched the ones who meet the sky.
You will blossom in every direction,
giving the fruit of knowledge as you go.
Seekers of wisdom, may you go forward into the light.
May all the seeds and corn you plant
bring forward the crops that will feed the thousands.
May your words ring out like the song of the sacred
bird issuing joy in everything to everything.
May your hearts and your burdens be light.

* * *

As Talocka Chooka's essence faded from view, a new energy pattern began to take shape. Round in his presence and soft in its approach, an immense tiger slowly appeared in front of me. His magnificent blue eyes and white fur were unlike anything I had ever viewed. As tears gathered in the corners of his large eyes, a feeling of love surrounded me. The gentle sound reverberating through his body pounded within my own, and the strength of his courage became mine. Etherically united in a peaceful embrace, his thoughts became my words as I gave his message.

Sar-ron

[Loud Purring.] I am Sar-ron, the white Bengal tiger. I have been chosen as speaker for all the animals. The white tiger is representative of the beauty of the heavenly animal kingdom. My kind is leaving the planet soon, but we have much to leave behind in the form of knowledge about keeping the animals alive...the ones that choose to remain. The yellow Bengals are also leaving, some due to poaching, but many have simply lost heart and can no longer find a mate to start their families or continue their journeys on the Earth plane.

We were very happy you came, that you touched us and you purred with us. Purr with me now so that I can hear you again. *[All purring.]* That's the sound of joy to all of us.

We hope we did not hurt you as we rolled and wrestled with each of you. It was such fun...like a game. It was like meeting and hugging long-lost friends.

As you rode on our backs in your etheric form, we showed you the splendor of the jungles, of the forests, of the world of the animal creatures: the snakes, birds, and monkeys; the toucans, pandas, and panthers; the cheetahs, lions, giraffes, and hippos—all sacred animals of the Earth. There are too many to name.

It has been so long since mankind has been in its highest form. We do not hunt man, and we do not attack unless provoked. We survive only for love, joy, and the opportunity to co-exist with our own and our human brothers and sisters.

In the past there were many human populations who enjoyed being in our presence, but they never took our claws, fangs, eyes, or muzzles for adornment. We lived long lives then, and it was not the quality of our fur that appealed to them, but the quality of our life. We lived in complete harmony with human beings in earlier times and we do not understand why they have not allowed us to be in freedom now.

We do not wish to leave...we do not want to go...but when the Creator has called us home, we must. There is a planet waiting; one where man has not been in existence, one where we will be free to have families and live out our lifespan the way the Creator has deemed.

We do not want you to feel guilty or be in pain for the acts of cruelty against us from others. We honor all life and each other, and we cherish that you shed our tears.

Your voices, your love, your touch have awakened the animals to the true understanding of what love is...that man and woman can be kind...that they are thinking of us, praying for us, and healing us. We wish all people would do this. They may not know that the tiger species overviews all animal life on Earth. We will wait, we will listen, we will watch; for the true language of the mind of man is very honest...very sweet...and if he can change his thoughts, he can save us all.

We look forward to the next time when we shall run and play and wrestle and ride. We kiss each of you with our large tongues. We honor you and know you feel the same way about us.

Until our paths meet again, Sar-ron. [All purring.]

* * *

As the essence of the tiger bounded off into the jungle, the total darkness behind my eyes drew me further in, searching for the flicker of light I knew must be there. The distant pounding of tribal drums gathered and grew inside, forcing me to tap out the rhythm with my feet. As the rumbling came closer, the glow from a distant ring of fire lit the night sky. A thousand stars sprinkled down onto the quiet desert and the booming voice of a tall, strong yet kind being engulfed me. Wearing a lion's mane around his neck and standing on one leg, with only bare arms and legs showing behind his large shield, he tapped out powerful repetitions with his spear. As this force proceeded through me, my own voice became his.

Chief Algunda

Aw-ta-hum-boo-oo-ta. I am Chief Al-gun-da from the Masai. I lived on the Earth plane for 300 years as a warrior in the great continent now known as Africa. At that time, AD 1200, we lived in the mountains and valleys not far from Kenya.

People of the Earth awaken. Hear the sound, the drumming of your hearts. Let your heartbeat be the world. Let your movements be the lungs of life. Watatooga!

Reconnect to your spirit life. The messages from the society in which you live are not the laws of the Universe.

I speak of the place where we all once lived—of the tundra and the plains...with all the great animals. The garnering of this energy is what you all need now. The spirit of freedom, along with the divinity of physicality in man and beast, has always been in the lion. I give to you a gift of lion energies.

E-M-P-O-W-E-R yourselves in the way of the lion. Even though the Masai are silent warriors, their power comes from knowing that they are like the lion they hunt, the lion they seek. The life you seek, you are; for if you do not believe that, you can never draw the life you seek to you. The king of the jungle has earned his title through patience, through knowing, through purpose.

Say it out loud. E-M-P-O-W-E-R. Even the tiny ants are empowered because they feel it, because they know it. It has nothing to do with size or proximity to region. Territory is one of the things that all animal species know. And yet your territories go beyond this world into the star systems, the realms beyond, the time of dreaming, and into the time of death.

Become warriors yourselves. Go out among those who do not know their territory and share what you can about the spirit realms, the kingdom of the animals, the star brothers, and about the lion's heart.

E-N-E-R-G-Y comes not only from this thing called food that you ingest, but it also comes from the essence of genuine energy, of loving life. Some of you have been trying to avoid it; however, you cannot avoid L-I-V-I-N-G. You may feel that where we are on this side is much more exciting, but living on Earth is where you learn the art of life. It is a great fish pond in the middle of an oasis. You have broken the boundaries of the fear of what eternity is and will graduate and go to realms where others dare not go.

We were with you during the talk at the fire. I watched your souls rise up to meet me and you asked, 'Why are the Masai so tall?'

And I answered, 'It is so we can touch the nearest star.'

I leave you now in the peacefulness of your thoughts, and one day I shall be with you on the Serengeti Plain and we shall dance together in the firelight.

* * *

Filled with exuberance, Rojo exclaimed, "Your spirit lesson for this evening has been completed. All the beings that initiated this meeting thank you for your participation. We hope you received the knowledge you've been searching for. It's not every day a rock can introduce so many wise and reverent beings in unison. Thank you for inviting, recording, and listening to their stories. You have spread the word and unearthed the buried treasure—a treasure filled with wisdom, knowledge, and power. Willingness is the key that opens the path to wisdom."

12

Crying Rock

Chief Algunda had mentioned that our world has a heart, and now the rocks were saying the same thing. On our last evening, Moha, Rojo's rock friend, shared a tearful farewell.

Moha

We are grateful for every beat of your hearts, and that is what we count when you are here...not time, nor energy, nor the placement of your human flesh. Your heartbeats have been collected in the Great Hall of the All Knowing. Each time we wish to think about you, we merely listen to the special heartbeat that fills the area of Sedona from the moment you arrive to the moment you leave.

All beings everywhere—animal, mineral, human, and even extra-terrestrial—know that your hearts go out to each living thing. There is a unique sound that comes when you arrive, and it will be quiet when you leave.

The rocks at the canyon you drove through today were crying. There were streams of water seeping from where there should be none. You have touched this area. You have given it feeling and life, leaving only beauty as you found it.

We have felt this deep connection with human beings only one other time here and that was with the Anasazi. You remind us of their presence. Your heartbeat matches theirs, and the rocks cry when you come and they cry when you leave.

Rojo prefers not to come through tonight. He does not want you to see your little rock friend cry. He will greet you when you are safely home. He wishes you great love...he wishes you everything you want...and most of all, he thanks you.

Goodnight, dear friends.

* * *

It was our last precious day in Sedona. The channeling from Moha the night before expressed gratitude for our combined presence there. Gifting us with a final farewell, she instructed us to return to the canyon near the newly formed vortex where we would find Crying Rock.

We had a promise to keep that final day as well. Patricia had been asked by a friend to return a bird-shaped rock to Sedona. The owner felt the rock was homesick, and Rojo confirmed its loneliness for its friends and relatives at the base of Bell Rock. This propitious deed was postponed until the last day because the well-loved rock, "Bird," had become part of our family, traveling everywhere with us.

Something had happened on this trip. We couldn't exactly put our fingers on it, but things were different somehow. The communication level of the rocks had changed. They were warmer, friendlier, and even more loving than before. But now we had been informed they were crying—a sign of thanks to show how much our presence meant to them. We had received channeling with instructions before, but this time it seemed incredible, if not impossible, to locate a rock...crying. We didn't know what to expect.

We followed Moha's directions, going back along the dusty road we'd driven the day before, speeding past bicyclists and pink jeeps in our rental car; kicking up dust and bouncing over the paveless road, our eyes darting, searching the rocks for signs of a tear.

Maybe the channeling hadn't been clear. Perhaps Moha was referring to a road sign or the name of a canyon. I was beginning to fear that our week might end on a low note if we weren't able to find what we'd been told was waiting for us.

As we turned the hairpin curve and proceeded up a hill, we couldn't believe our eyes. There before us, in the middle of a huge shale of rock, was a giant teardrop. We were speechless and awed as we viewed the dampened red soil and wet droplets trickling out of the mountainside. We bounded out of the car and ran to touch Crying Rock's tears.

I'm convinced that if it weren't for our snapshots, we still wouldn't believe what we saw. It was a miracle! Not magic, whim, or imagination— but real, tangible evidence of Earth communication. We were delighted and honored that rocks wanted to share what human beings sometimes take for granted...love.

Had we seen it all? Hardly. This was just a slight preview of what was to come.

As for "Bird," he was returned home to the shade of a juniper tree, surrounded by his insect friends, just smiling his little rock smile.

And the three of us, with our hearts full, reluctantly waved goodbye to Bird, Rojo, and the beauty of Sedona.

13

Earthwatcher

The memories slowly faded throughout the months after we were immersed in Sedona's magic. My mind, like a colorful scrapbook, continuously reviewed the mystery of each precious day spent there. But something was missing. I had the uneasy feeling that complete closure had not yet taken place. What could it be? Was another trip on the agenda? Had we missed some information? For the life of me, I couldn't shake that eerie, heavy energy.

It was the middle of the night. Sleep had evaded me as my mind replayed the events of our three trips. Suddenly…BANG!…a loud cracking sound above my head jolted me back to the present. It was a noise so loud I couldn't ignore the butterflies in my solar plexus. My digital clock…once again…showed 3:33 a.m. I sensed something very unusual was about to make its presence known. The feeling was desperate and intense.

As I checked in with my guidance to validate the level of positive energy, I learned only that I would have to knuckle down, pay attention, and respond accordingly.

Just then, a distant voice instructed me. "Remain awake. You must record the narrative regarding the future of the Earth."

"But I'm frightened of what you might tell me." My thoughts raced to many others who had predicted doom and destruction. Then Rojo's familiar lyrical voice entered my consciousness to offer reassurance. "I am here. I am here. Earthwatcher wishes to tell the people about their future."

It was becoming an imaginative chess match and checkmate had just been declared. It seemed I had no choice but to grope my way to the computer through the darkness of early morning.

"But Rojo," I protested, "I thought you would be telling me about the future.

The friendly voice peeked through again. "I will be with you as the messages come, but it is not for me to say. Don't be afraid. Earthwatcher is wiser and much more knowing than even the rocks and all the other consciousnesses of this planet."

I could feel my resistance begin to set in, for the vibrations of this entity were serious and condescending. This was not going to be a comfy fireside chat. "All right, Earthwatcher, I'm ready. What can you tell me?"

The voice of the elder came through loud and clear. "I will tell you the outcome of this world in which you live, even if you do not welcome my words. The future, my seer, is one of a sunless sky and a barren plain. The mountains, trees, and oceans will cease to exist. It has already begun— the deionization of your planet by electricity and other waves of energy brought into the environment by greedy men who are planning to live in the sky and not on the land.

"The places in which man will reside in the future world will emulate those thoughts of your science fiction writers. Man will have forgotten his fellow man and will live by and with the machines he has created. Little contact of the physical kind will disrupt his relationships, and fear of intimacy will be your next disease process.

"Domed cities will block the decay and dying of the plant, animal, and mineral life, long replaced by artificial means and forgotten, like fruit rotting on the vine.

"The money changers of the world will control the minds of most people, except those who choose not to conform. These rebels will be forced to live upon the dying rocks and the sinking ocean.

"Man will look for other planets to colonize, and once again your world will return to dust and your people will no longer know one another.

"Artificial intelligence will be in charge of even the gene pools of brothers and sisters, and one will no longer know the stories of previous generations. The great stories of the Earth will be wiped away with the flick of a switch or the push of a button, and you shall not know your brother.

"You will all appear perfect, and you will never be accepted by another unless you have the 'proper' genetic structures. Beauty of the physical self will be the medicine of the future and those who do not look equal will have artificial features provided through technology.

"It will no longer be a world of kindness and understanding, but one of like kind. The ability to get close and touch one another will be reserved for only the affluent. They may not even choose to communicate for fear of contamination.

"Zones will exist throughout the world and you may never ever leave your dwelling, let alone know what the outside of the planet looks like. Your travels will be artificially provided and all will be locked into non-truth.

"The wheels of the great plan to deceive the beings who are in human form are already in motion, sucked in by a giant whirlpool of tempting gadgets, appliances, and devices.

"The allure of more free time and less costly means of support will be everywhere, even on the lips of your offspring. Children will be a rare commodity and the population will be strictly enforced. Man will lose his desire to be mother and father, and by doing so will lose the most precious part of himself—the ability to love.

"'Get all you can before it's gone' will be the slogan of the conglomerates, too many for you to even know who they are. Individual freedom will be a thing of the past, and crime will equal its punishment to the extreme.

"The wandering spirits of the Earth will help to destroy the atmosphere by causing nature to evoke destruction, and the angels will no longer be seen. The ageless spirits of the Earth—sun, moon, and sky—will cry for each other, and mankind shall not remember their names.

"The animals will leave the planet first, through disease and eventually extinction, and the insects will devour the food supply.

"Great famine shall rid the Earth of those who are feeble or penniless, and the multitudes will call it 'nature's way' and will not tell the truth of the collusion of the money changers to make it so.

"The rivers will no longer supply the water or the fish. They will be dry and lost to the desert where plant life can no longer flourish to sustain the many.

"There will be great rumors of destruction from the sky, evoked by those in power to keep the human race inside so they do not witness the putrefaction of their surroundings. The ones who live in the sky will be born there and know nothing of the world of their ancestors.

"And what of the day and night? The nights will grow longer due to pollutants and the destruction caused by harmful rays to the protective layers of the atmosphere. Man will cry out for the coolness of the night, and the moneychangers will make it so.

"Life will begin in the sterile dishes you now use for helping life take form, and co-creation will no longer be necessary. When this happens, self-destruction is the ultimate outcome.

"This is where your beautiful planet is headed if you do not change your own minds and take care of the future. Do not ask how to do this. Let your hearts be your guide. Stand up for what is the truth and do not forget to look the other way when the moneychangers dangle and twinkle their wares before you. Let them go on by, for your world's soul is at stake.

"Did you not know that your world has a soul? It has a heart and mind as well. It is your great brother and sister, mother and father, made in the image of your own true self. Honor yourselves so that you may honor the World, the Universe, and The Great Forever.

"Go in peace, honor, and light. The love is yours to keep or dispose of, depending upon your sacred will. But have the will to at least choose.

"In your thoughts and dreams, Earthwatcher."

*   *   *

The words stung and would not stop coming. The keyboard began to blur as the solitude of such a landscape formed in my mind—visions of unfathomable chaos and nothingness—picturing a lifeless, soulless world. I saw fierce winds cover the face of the planet and a desolate Earth span as far as the eye could see. Even the mountains and the rocks had crumbled into dust, revealing the shiny, domed cities and the silence of it all.

That's what was so disturbing: the silence. It was a silence so vast that nothing could penetrate it.

Would this be the outcome for the world we know as our home? I could only imagine the faces of children who might read these words. Should I censor the message of Earthwatcher? Did I dare edit this possible future like a poorly formed sentence to best be forgotten?

"NO," Rojo warned. "To do so would be an act of 'non-truth.' If you tell them, warn them, give them the knowledge, it will be their choice to accept or reject. Give them a chance. It is all we ask."

*   *   *

A hundred questions flashed across my brain. Did it have to be this way? Was there something we could do to change the outcome? Was there an alternative if we would turn everything around right now? I must contact Earthwatcher again. This guide was new to me, and I couldn't tell if it was an Indian spirit or an energy formation.

I knew there had to be a way I could connect with the future. I had recently discovered that music, the universal language of all time, had the ability to immediately reach certain beings. I would put on my headphones and listen to the sounds of the winds and waters, and then hope for the best.

"Earthwatcher, I need to know more. I have more questions. Will you answer me, please?" The music seemed to go on forever. "Rojo, please help me contact Earthwatcher. I need to know if there is more."

Then the words slowly began. "You have summoned me, my sister, to reveal the alternate outcome. There are always choices in the universe and nothing is set in stone. Therefore, the wisdom to ask for an option shows the interest you have in life. We are required to answer and tell the truths of what we know if you have the consciousness to request it.

"The future can be different if the souls of the Earth align with the consciousness of all life everywhere. I can access groups of human thinking, including the group known to you as light workers.

"In the quest to find your true destiny, you must freely choose peace and harmony above all else. In this way, your future world can result in an entirely different form.

"But the light workers are not the majority of thought-producing beings at this time in your history. The previous view of the future was projected, in part, by the limited thoughts in the minds of most humans. Because of their sheer quantity, these people are presently responsible for the projected outcome. There are still not enough light workers to create your perception of the ideal world of the future."

I begged, "But Earthwatcher, perhaps if you could describe a possible world. Through this story, you might help us change such a non-conscious outcome."

"It is not up to us one way or the other. We are impartial observers of your souls' desires. But since you are requesting it, allow us to show you the vision of those working toward a better world."

At last a breakthrough. It had taken only an hour to discover what I really wanted to know...that there could be an alternate course. I closed my eyes and let the process unfold.

*   *   *

"It is I, Earthwatcher. The future will be a self-contained environment with all species interactive and respectful of each other's needs. There are new mountains, volcanoes, and rivers birthing themselves on the planet. They are unmarred by human contact and left alone to cultivate nature's true task of creating land for the collective masses of people who will inhabit it in the millions of years to come.

"The human beings of the planet are creating perpetual life and an abundance of knowledge for future generations; for they, too, may someday wish to again incarnate into this world of light.

"The cities of the past no longer exist. The new cities are of respectable size, and some are constructed with natural Earth materials that provide optimum living conditions. These dwellings literally recycle themselves after the lives of their residents are physically over.

"The sea, with its natural rhythms, will provide energy for the planet. It will be harnessed and used for energy to provide light and the many comforts of living. Everything, however, is more simple, usable for all seasons, and convertible in its nature.

"Vehicles are smooth and streamlined, powered by the ultraviolet rays of the sun; and the air is, at last, clean. Children are cared for and honored by only those who understand and love them; and for those who cannot, there are several alternative options.

"People will not fear each other's words or actions, for their thoughts will intermingle with great understanding. Disputes will be resolved by those who start them, and forgiveness will be on the lips of all, for they will seek to understand.

"Contact with other civilizations throughout the universe will now be possible, and man will be free to explore worlds beyond time, space, and imagination. Technology is available for those who wish to explore, not exploit. Freedom is still the work of the human will, but a responsible will and forethought of true freedom will prevail.

"Those who wish for alternative living will be given choices. By doing so they will be able to construct their own life patterns in the houses of the sky or on other worlds. Man will again be revered by his thoughts, and the angelic kingdom can once more be among you upon the Earth.

"The animals, in communion with the insects and the human beings, will take their place among the bearers of harmony and love. The sea will remain blue, and the clouds and wind call out my name and yours.

"The creative works of man will now be limitless, and what is dreamed of can become a reality in all dimensional forms. Man will no longer subject his thinking to the idea of mere existence, but will contemplate his true nature of self-power and self-love. All of the consciousness of human beings will become motivated by the co-creative power of their love for each other, themselves, and the universe.

"In your thoughts and dreams, Earthwatcher."

Earthwatcher's Daily Suggestions for Creating a Better World

1. Contact your own consciousness with a moment of silence each morning

2. Take a moment to thank nature for supporting you

3. Ask a question and receive an answer from a plant, animal, or mineral and share that wisdom with a friend

4. Implement a daily routine of releasing old fears and patterns by surrendering them to the universe in writing

5. Carry with you a form of nature (rock, leaf, flower, or shell) that reminds you of your connection to Earth

6. Acknowledge others with love, kindness, and support

7. Emit a sense of trust, patience, and openness to everyone you meet

8. Envision the world as you expect it to be

14

Omega

We had heard it all, from Rojo's cosmic tour through the vortexes of Sedona to humanity's potential demise. And, in between, our own story...lives paralleling the existence of everything. Ours was a scenario shot in black and white...the yin and the yang, negative and positive, polarity in a nutshell.

"You've got it," Rojo's little voice rejoiced. "Remember? Life is like a bright, shiny button. It is also like the dark, displaced button. When life is removed from its purpose by an act of circumstance, it always retains two or more options. We have tried to show that both are relative...by the fact that it is up to you to choose if and how. Only you can decide what the ultimate choice will be.

"The first button was returned to you by the tour guide, even though you did not recognize it. You hesitated at first to accept it for you did not realize it belonged to you. When you accepted it, you made a choice...one of many; but still, you made it. What you did with it then, was completely left up to you.

"The dark button found you also, but you also found it. This created a mutual-consent process that was put into motion. You were not as attracted to this button for it was dull and weathered, but you instinctively picked it up, not knowing what it held for you.

"Both buttons can either be used or thrown away. These buttons are symbols of every aspect of living, providing multiple choices. Their destiny is dependent upon your choice. If you choose, you may sew them onto cloth so they can hold things together, or you may simply discard them if you do not see their value as a metaphor.

"It is the same in life through the cycles of all living things. Synchronistic acts of curiosity bring you to new moments of time and space. This is a miracle of sorts, yet every day you exist is another miracle set in motion. Your acts are choices—whether the world shall exist in a more perfect state, or whether it will find its way to Earthwatcher's end.

"Do you know that if you count the number of buttons in the world, they would exceed the number of people available to wear them? This entire journey has been to invite you to perceive that which is already around you. Yet, most humans do not equate their everyday world with the importance each atom, molecule, quark, or button holds for them. It is your timeless consciousness that meets life with either a wide or a narrow view. We are here to open your minds to the alternate consciousness that makes up our universe.

"You are the only ones who can perceive your own world and the multitude of choices that lie therein. Choose wisely. Hopefully you will find joy, peace, and love. We can only ask you to love your world as we love ours; for we, in essence, are indeed one. Without one another, we cannot live in a universe of choice or experience the vastness of love...the love that exists in all universes. Love's vibration and frequency are one and the same. We all share molecules of this frequency in proportion to the equilibrium of our existence.

"Will you continue to share yours? We are waiting for you to accept your buttons or discard them. As Earthwatcher has suggested, the choice is ultimately...yours.

"As it was in the beginning...so it shall be in the end."

*"Once upon a time
in a dimension near you...
a new planet is forming,"
Rojo's little voice said.*

About the Author

Rosemary Brown Sanders is a nationally known intuitive, numerologist, and certified hypnotherapist. Known as the "Psychic's Psychic" for her accuracy in predicting for other psychics, she brings to this project 20 years of inspirational study in the field of metaphysics. She is producer and host of her own talk-radio program in Monterey, California and offers workshops, classes, audiotapes, and remote viewing to hundreds of people.

Rosemary is able to channel a wide variety of beings, including animals, rocks, guides, and angels. She also perceives information about past lives, forecasting accurately for clients about relationship and career issues. Her articles have appeared in *Sedona Journal of Emergence* and *Harper's Magazine.* She is devoted to the exploration of principles for spiritual and personal success. Her goal is to inspire and motivate people to tap into their own natural abilities.

To Contact the Author

Order audiotapes or books at address below:

*Rock People of Sedona audiotape—$12.00
Side 1—Visualizations by *Moha and the City of Light,* the *Seeker's Prayer,* and the *Prayer to Creation* read by Rosemary Brown Sanders
Side 2—Rosemary Brown Sanders channeling *Rojo*

*Angel Whispers tape series (includes 40 affirmation cards)—$21.95
Two tapes include four visualizations:
   Angel Whispers
   Body Talk—Healing Affirmations
   Renewing Relationships with Your Inner Child
   Manifesting On All Levels

Please include shipping and handling:
   One item—$3.00
   Each additional item—$1.00
   Tax included on all items.

Rosemary Brown Sanders
P. O. Box 222872
Carmel, CA 93922-2872

To receive information about private consultations,
contact Sally Winkleblack at:
Telephone: 831-373-4676
Email: Cosmicornr@aol.com
WebPage: www.rosemarybrownsanders.com

To order additional copies of *The Rock People of Sedona,* call 1-877-288-4737 or email custservice@iuniverse.com.

Made in the USA
Las Vegas, NV
27 July 2023

75322109R00069